AN ORPHAN CALLED CHRISTMAS

Victorian Romance

FAYE GODWIN

Tica House
Publishing
Sweet Romance that Delights and Enchants!

Copyright © 2022 by Faye Godwin

All rights reserved.

No part of this book may be reproduced in any form or by any electronic or mechanical means, including information storage and retrieval systems, without written permission from the author, except for the use of brief quotations in a book review.

PERSONAL WORD FROM THE AUTHOR

DEAREST READERS,

I'm so delighted that you have chosen one of my books to read. I am proud to be a part of the team of writers at Tica House Publishing. Our goal is to inspire, entertain, and give you many hours of reading pleasure. Your kind words and loving readership are deeply appreciated.

I would like to personally invite you to sign up for updates and to become part of our **Exclusive Reader Club**—it's completely Free to Join! I'd love to welcome you!

Much love,

Faye Godwin

CLICK HERE to Join our Reader's Club and to Receive Tica House Updates!

https://victorian.subscribemenow.com/

CONTENTS

PART I

CHAPTER 1

BEULAH ELLIS REMINDED herself that she had done this before. It wasn't easy, not with Dovie's screams of pain and panic echoing around the room. The little girl lay in a tangle of sweat-soaked sheets in the room that had once belonged to her mother, decades ago, and her shrieks threatened to lift the roof from the cottage.

"It's all right, pet. It's all right." Beulah smoothed sweaty hair back from Dovie's face with one hand, gripping the girl's hand in the other.

Dovie fell back against her pillows, gasping, her body trembling violently, her hand clasped over the swollen curve of her abdomen. "What's happening, Granny?" she gasped.

Beulah looked into Dovie's wide, milky-blue eyes. Fifteen years old. She was just a bairn herself, but like it or not, she and Beulah would be bringing a child into the world this night. Beulah could only pray that the baby's mother, a child herself, would survive it.

She wondered how to explain. How to tell Dovie that what she might have believed was innocent, forbidden fun with that handsome lad who worked in her parents' garden had led to this. Had Carol never discussed such things with her daughter?

Before Beulah could answer, another shriek tore from Dovie's lungs. The girl's body folded, doubling with the force of the contraction, her knees drawing up, her scream growing louder and louder and reaching a desperate pitch as her skinny legs curled in pain.

"Hush, hush," Beulah soothed, stroking Dovie's forehead as the girl's trembling grip crushed the little bones in Beulah's hand.

"What's *happening*?" Dovie screamed.

Beulah pulled back Dovie's skirt, saw the purplish crown of the baby beginning to emerge.

"You're having your baby, just like we said," she told her.

"Right now?" Dovie panted, sweat pouring down her cheeks. "*Now*? Why does it hurt so much?"

"Yes. Right now," said Beulah. "Be brave now, pet." She released the girl's hand, took up her position at the bottom of the bed. "And when I tell you to push, do it."

Sobbing, Dovie fell back against her pillows, her tiny body heaving wildly with agony and terror. Outside, Beulah could hear something. Singing. She looked through the window. Sure enough, in the street below this attic that had been Carol's room and was now Dovie's, she could see a string of boys and girls in neat white robes striding down the street. They carried candles that cast golden haloes around them as they walked.

The window was open a crack to allow a kiss of cold air to touch Dovie's fevered skin, and the song rose softly through the crack, bringing a note of peace into the room that still echoed Dovie's screams.

"O holy night, the stars are brightly shining. It is the night of our dear Savior's birth."

Beulah closed her eyes, savoring the sweet sound. "Hear that, Dovie," she whispered. "Listen to that carol."

For a moment, the girl calmed, listening, as the song continued.

"Long lay the world in sin and error pining, 'till he appeared, and the soul felt its worth."

"Listen, Dovie," Beulah said, turning to her. "It was a winter night like this one, just as cold, and far more lonely, that our

9

Saviour came into the world." She fixed the girl with a steady look. "His mother was no older than you, you know. Perhaps even younger. But God gave her the strength to bring the Holy Babe into this world, and He will give you the strength, also."

Dovie let out a sob, tears rolling down her cheeks. "I don't know what you're talking about." The end of the sentence became a scream as another contraction seized her.

Beulah barely had time to wonder if her parents had even sent Dovie to Sunday school when the baby's head was slipping toward her, the face all scrunched and purplish in a way that frightened her a little even though she had done this before.

"Push, Dovie," she ordered. "*Push*."

"I can't," Dovie sobbed.

"Push," Beulah commanded. Dovie pushed and with screams and struggles and little inches of progress at a time, the baby finally slid into Beulah's arms. She caught it in a towel and rubbed its face briskly, working the fluid away from its mouth and nose, briskly towelling the tiny ribcage.

She was rewarded instantly with a tiny mouth that opened wide and sucked in a long, rattling breath. Then the baby's cry echoed through the room, long and wailing and healthy.

"It's a girl." Beulah found herself smiling down at the babe in her arms as she briskly took care of the cord and wrapped the baby in its towel. "Dovie, it's a beautiful little girl."

Dovie had collapsed back against her pillow, sobbing in a haze of pain and exhaustion, but at least her cheeks were pink, and her breaths came strongly. She was too young to have done this, of course, but Beulah knew she would live. After all, up until a few weeks ago, Dovie had lived well in her parents' house.

"Come, Dovie." Beulah straightened, cradling the screaming baby in her arms. "Sit up and see your little girl."

Dovie struggled to sit. Beulah straightened the covers around her legs and sat down on the edge of the bed, smiling. "Look at her. It was all worth the pain. Here she is."

Dovie stared down at the baby. Still whimpering, the babe's cheeks were healthy pink now, and she was just beginning to open those dark-blue baby eyes. For an instant, a change crossed Dovie's hardened face, and her eyes softened long enough for her to reach out and touch the baby's cheek with her fingertip.

"Her name is Christmas," she murmured. "Because she was born on Christmas Day."

Beulah smiled. "Maybe something like Noelle would be better. Or Holly."

"No." Dovie's mouth flattened. "It's Christmas."

"All right." Beulah nodded. "She's your daughter."

Dovie's face shut down instantly. Her eyes hardened again, and she flung herself down in the bed, moaning with pain. "Take it away."

The harshness of the words slapped Beulah in the face. "Oh, pet, I know you're in pain, but—"

"I don't want it." Dovie's voice was cold and flat. She turned her face away. "Please. Take it away."

Beulah stared at her, heart hammering. She remembered her own pain after Carol was born, yet she had wanted that baby more than anything else in the world. But every woman was different, she reminded herself, and Carol had come when Beulah was twenty and married and longing for a child. It was different for poor, poor Dovie.

"All right," she said softly, cuddling the baby. "I'll bring her back a little later, when you're more ready."

Dovie made no response. Beulah stepped out of the attic and carried the baby into her own bedroom. Her husband, Roy, was out in the barn; he couldn't stand Dovie's screams. She gazed through the window at the little stone barn that squatted against the side of the snow-covered hill, the landscape of this countryside just outside London all whites and greys.

The carolers had moved on, but Beulah went on humming their carol.

O night divine, O night when Christ was born.

O night, O night, O night divine.

❦

BABY CHRISTMAS WHIMPERED, kicking her tiny legs in the crib that Roy had cobbled together from old bits of wood he'd found around the barn. Her tiny, skinny arms rose into the air, wobbling with weakness, and she let out another of her thin, ever-weakening cries.

"What ails the child, Beu?" Roy asked, leaning awkwardly over the crib. He had been a giant in his youth; even though stooped with age now, he still looked disproportionately tall for the tiny cottage kitchen. "She's fussin' something awful."

"Dovie still won't feed her." Beulah sighed. "I've given her a little warm milk and a beaten egg, but she needs her mother's milk."

"Poor lass." Roy grunted with sorrow, pulling up a three-legged stool and reaching into the crib to offer the baby one of his work-fattened fingers. "Stop fussin', little one. Your mama will see to you soon."

"She just needs her strength," said Beulah. She stood by the old woodstove, spooning broth into a bowl. It was only vegetable broth with a few bones in it, but it would do something. "She'll feel better once she's eaten, and then the baby can drink."

"Has she named the little thing?" Roy asked, tickling the baby's cheek.

The big man chuckled, his white-stubbled face creasing, and Beulah felt the same melting love within her that she had the day they married fifty years ago.

"Yes, she wants to name her Christmas." Beulah laughed.

"Aw, I think it's a good name," said Roy. "A little Christmas blessing, aren't you, pet?" He looked up at Beulah. "Can I go to see Dovie?"

"Not yet. I've cleaned her up, but she must feel shy." Beulah picked up the bowl and a spoon. "But I'll ask her now, when she's eaten."

"All right. I'll stay here with this little precious." Roy beamed down at baby Christmas. "Give her my love, will you?"

"Of course, dear." Beulah kissed his wrinkled cheek and mounted the steps to the attic slowly and stiffly, her aging knees complaining with every step. Puffing, she reached the door and froze.

The door was open, but Beulah was certain she had closed it behind her.

A sudden, terrifying suspicion plunged through Beulah's belly. "Dovie?" she called out, hurrying through the door.

The bed was empty, its new, fresh bedclothes rumpled. The glass of milk Beulah had put on the nightstand was untouched.

"Dovie." Beulah gasped. She set down the soup and looked around the tiny room, even crouching down despite her aching joints to peer under the bed. But it was empty. Dovie was gone.

Beulah's hands were shaking as she descended the steps into the kitchen. Roy stood in the doorway, cradling the baby in his big arms, and his face was grim.

"Gone?" he asked.

"Yes." Beulah sighed. "Oh, Roy, I don't know how it happened. I... I went out to get wood for the stove, while you were still in the barn. She must have slipped out then."

"I'll find her," Roy promised. He set the baby in Beulah's arms. "She can't have gone far."

The big man rushed out of the room, and Beulah sagged into her rocking chair, cradling the hungry babe. Christmas looked up at her with unfocused eyes, letting out a soft whimper, turning her head from side to side as she sought nourishment.

"I'm sorry, little one," Beulah whispered, hot tears running down her cheeks. "I've failed you both."

BEULAH TRUDGED through the deep snow, her shawl clutched tightly around her shoulders against the biting wind. Her boots sank so deep that snow found its way inside, nipping at her ankles and toes, making the ever-present pain a little worse with every step. But she kept going, raising a hand to shield her face from the driving wind and snow.

The past day and night had gone by in a blur. Roy had spent all night looking for Dovie, asking their neighbors for help. Even the Costigans, who could be tight-fisted, found something of Christmas love in their hearts and helped. But the girl had vanished like smoke into the sky. She was nowhere to be found.

Part of Beulah believed she'd come back for Christmas. But the baby was now twenty-four hours old and fading fast.

"We're not going to find her, dear," Roy had told her. "She doesn't want to be found. She's gone. It's our task to care for the baby now."

Beulah knew he was right, but her heart still ached for that poor, frightened girl. If only her parents—Beulah's own daughter, Carol, and that rich husband of hers—hadn't thrown Dovie out of the house when they had discovered her pregnancy, maybe this would never have happened. Now Dovie was out there alone and scared and in pain.

What had Beulah done wrong? Had she said something to make Dovie believe that she would find anything but love and acceptance in Beulah's arms? These felt like questions that would weigh upon her heart for all eternity.

Squinting against the driving snow, Beulah focused on the small house at the top of the hill. A thin wisp of smoke trailed from its chimney, and some disconsolate hens watched the blowing snow from a ramshackle henhouse cobbled together with scraps of wood. The house itself was little better, a wooden structure teetering slightly to one side. All of its windows except one was boarded up, and an air of utter neglect hung over the entire house, clinging to its roof with its missing shingles and howling through the gaps in its boards.

Fighting her way against the wind to the front door, Beulah raised a hand and knocked. The noise echoed hollowly through the house. She could hear a baby crying in a steady, constant wail.

The door swung open, and a scrawny, greasy woman glared at her. Her hair hung down around her face in unwashed ropes, and her apron was smeared with filth. A toddler clung to her skirt, surely no more than a year and a half old, its little head tipped back, weeping and weeping.

For a moment, Beulah's heart quailed at the thought of letting this woman anywhere near the baby. But she had no choice. "Mrs. Mackintosh?" she asked.

The woman gave her a loose-lipped stare. "That's me. And I ain't in the mood for visitors, so clear off." She stepped back.

"No, no. I'm not a visitor. I have a job for you. Money," Beulah shouted, even though her heart wobbled at the thought of spending even more of the money they didn't have.

The woman stopped at the sound of that magical word, her eyes widening. "Job? What kind of job?"

A collection of pale, dirty little faces peered around Mrs. Mackintosh at Beulah. There were so many of them that Beulah was momentarily speechless.

"There's ten," Mrs. Mackintosh barked. "Don't bother judgin' me. I wasn't the one who wanted all of them. My good-for-nothing husband wanted all of the brats, and now they've ruined us, having so many mouths to feed."

"I... I'm not judging." Beulah took a deep breath, blushing at the realization that she certainly was. "Mrs. Mackintosh, I understand you had a very tragic loss recently."

Mrs. Mackintosh's eyes narrowed. "I lost my baby. What of it?"

"Would you be able to nurse another child?" Beulah asked. "A very small baby. Born yesterday, on Christmas Day."

Mrs. Mackintosh sighed. "For money?"

"Yes." Beulah reached into her pocket for the pouch of precious coins and held it up, clinking them. "You'll be paid every week."

"The first week in advance." Mrs. Mackintosh crossed her arms.

Beulah looked down at the wailing toddler. Again, she hated the thought of the baby in this hard woman's arms, but the child needed milk to survive more than she needed another woman's kindness. Beulah could love her enough for both of them, she hoped.

"If you come with me at once, I will pay you the first week's wage right now," Beulah said.

CHAPTER 2

Six Years Later

CHRISSIE ELLIS LET out a burst of wild laughter as she ran across the snowy field. Despite the wind that clutched at her cheeks, her belly and chest and arms and legs all felt warm and glowing. Maybe that was because she was running or maybe it was because she was happy. Chrissie didn't know, and she didn't care right now; she just liked the warmth and the feeling of her shoes hitting the snow and the laughter that filled her chest.

"It's going to get you, Princess Chrissie." The piping voice belonged to a young boy running right beside her, each of his strides matching hers. He had blowing brown curls and big brown eyes that sparkled with excitement. "It's swooping to get you."

"No, no." Chrissie squealed with laughter, throwing up her arms to ward off the imaginary dragon that was plunging from the sky toward her.

"It's coming for you. Its claws are going to get you," Jonah Costigan yelled, holding out his hands like talons.

"Save me, Prince Jonah, save me!" Chrissie gasped, throwing herself to the ground. She landed face-first in the soft, fluffy snow of the field and lay there, giggling, as Jonah hurled himself over her. "Prince Jonah is catching it," he yelled, arms flailing. "I've got it—oh—oops."

Chrissie sat up, laughing ever louder as Jonah rolled down the little bank toward the stream, which lay still and grey and frozen between its banks. Jonah tumbled to a halt on the stream and skidded some way across the ice, laughing.

"You fought it, Prince Jonah, and you won." She scrambled to her feet, brushing snow from her mittens and scarf. "You killed the dragon."

Jonah sat up, chuckling, his cheeks rosy beneath his curls. "I *slayed* the dragon. You don't kill dragons—you *slay* them."

"You slayed it," Chrissie cheered. She stumbled down the bank toward him.

"Stay off the ice, Chrissie." Jonah held out his hand. "It might not be strong enough for both of us."

Chrissie waited obediently at the edge of the stream. Jonah was nine years old, after all, three years older than she was; he knew everything.

She reached out and grabbed his arm as he slipped his way to the edge, and they stepped out onto the bank. "Now what?" Chrissie asked. "Does all of Fairyland rejoice over the dragon's death?"

"Yes," said Jonah, "and all the fairies can dance in the moonlit glades again because he'll never eat their fairy cows again." He grinned.

Chrissie beamed up at him. Jonah always came up with the very best fairy tales. "All hail the hero, Prince Jonah," she cheered.

"And the heroine, Princess Chrissie, the cleverest and bravest," Jonah said.

Chrissie laughed. She didn't think she was that clever and brave, but Princess Chrissie was. She was a fairy heroine, Jonah always told her, with all the powers of Christmas. She wasn't sure what those were, but she liked the sound of them.

In the distance, the church bell tolled sonorously. Chrissie stood still, counting the tolling sounds on her fingers. Four o' clock.

"Time to go home," she said.

"That's right." Jonah held out a mittened hand. "Come on. I'll walk you back home."

"Thank you," Chrissie said nicely, just like Nana Beulah had taught her. She took his hand, and he towed her up the bank and across the field.

It was Farmer Green's field, a nice old chap who never minded if the children played in it, and it looked right over the village. Chrissie smiled at the sight of the village. The houses were all very small; the fancy houses were just over the next fell, where the lords and ladies lived. But these people were farmers and tinkers and grocers and tailors, and they were ordinary folk. Yet this year, they had set up a big old Christmas tree in the market square after John the grocer's pine tree had blown over in a November storm. It looked quite splendid from up here, where Chrissie couldn't see all of its bent branches, all wrapped up in ribbons. Golden candlelight glowed in all of the windows.

"O Christmas tree, O Christmas tree, how lovely are thy branches," Chrissie sang in time with her skipping as Jonah led her through the stile and onto the main street leading through the village.

Jonah giggled. "Keep singing, Princess Chrissie. Your voice enchants the world."

Chrissie chuckled. "You're so silly, Jonah. I'm not Princess Chrissie now. Just Chrissie."

Jonah's eyes sparkled. "Well, you sing like an angel, Just Chrissie."

Chrissie's peals of laughter rang over the snow-dusted market square.

"I think we have roast chicken for Christmas Eve tonight." Jonah's eyes gleamed. "I don't think we've had a whole roast chicken for three months." He sighed. "I wish we could have a whole goose like the rich folks."

"Nana Beulah says that we're very lucky to have roast chickens," said Chrissie. "Nana Beulah says that everyone's got a different lot in life, and it's good to be grateful for yours if you have a bite to eat and a roof over your head."

Jonah laughed. "I bet Nana Beulah would still like a roast goose."

"I don't know what goose is like. Maybe it's horrid," said Chrissie. "Maybe it tastes like ground-up liver and onions." She made a gagging noise.

Jonah laughed. "Maybe it does—though I like liver and onions."

They had almost reached the Christmas tree now, and Chrissie saw that a few of the other neighborhood children were playing under the tree itself. She immediately slowed, tugging at Jonah's arm. She didn't want to talk to the farmers' children; Farmer Green was nice, but his children—and his neighbors' children—were nasty at times.

But then she saw that Peter, Farmer Green's oldest child, was holding something marvelous in his hand—something brightly colorful. Pulling Jonah forward, she gasped. "Look. It's a top. It's a beautiful top."

"It *is* beautiful," said Jonah.

The top was blue and green and red and very shiny, and Peter whipped it expertly on the cobblestones so that it spun like something magical, flashing in the pale, wispy sunlight. Chrissie couldn't help getting closer. She inched forward, gazing at it, her mouth wide open, awed by its beauty.

"It's so beautiful," she gasped.

At once, Peter snatched up the top, glaring at her. "Go away. We don't want to play with you."

Chrissie retreated a step, hanging on to Jonah's hand. "I'm just looking," she mumbled.

Peter scoffed at her. "Well, don't look. Just go away."

"Yes, we don't want to play with the likes of you," said one of the other boys. "Mama says you're dirty and rotten."

Chrissie gasped, tears stinging her eyes.

"Now you take that back." Jonah let go of her hand and made fists of his own.

"It's the truth," Peter said, his eyes glittering. "Mama says the same thing. She says that she shouldn't even have been born. She doesn't have a mama and papa like normal children."

Chrissie sobbed.

"Say that again and I'll box your ears for you," Jonah roared.

Peter snorted. "I'd like to see you try."

"Jonah, don't." Chrissie grabbed at his sleeve, still sobbing. "He's so big. He'll hurt you."

"I don't care," said Jonah fiercely. "He wants his ears boxed."

"I want to go home," Chrissie sobbed. "Please, Jonah, just take me home."

Jonah glared at him with narrowed eyes, then took Chrissie's hands. "Don't listen to their rubbish, Chrissie. Let's go home."

But the sound of the other children's jeering followed Chrissie and Jonah all the way to Nana Beulah and Papa Roy's house at the end of the street.

⊙⅋⊙

JUST AS NANA BEULAH had promised, Christmas Eve dinner was very, very special. It wasn't soup or bread and cheese or even salted fish or sausages. Instead, Chrissie's mouth watered as she watched Nana Beulah taking a whole roast chicken out of the oven. The roast chicken was an old rooster that had been butchered earlier, and it was more bones than flesh, but it was golden and covered with dried herbs from Nana Beulah's garden, and it looked wonderful. Nestling in a bed of golden roast potatoes, it even had some roast carrots with it, and a gravy that Papa Roy poured very carefully into the mug that they used instead of a gravy-boat.

"There's even some butter, thanks to the kind little milk-maid," said Nana Beulah, beaming with pride as she set the golden pat of butter down in the middle of the table.

Chrissie smiled around at the cottage kitchen. It wasn't very big, but she had helped Nana Beulah to hang wreaths and garlands everywhere, and it was bright with candles and holly berries.

"I love Christmas," she said.

Papa Roy grinned at her, his blue eyes sparkling. "I love Christmas, too. She's a very sweet little girl."

Chrissie giggled. "Nobody really calls me that, Papa Roy."

"Well, I still think she's very sweet, don't you?" Papa Roy reached under the table and tickled her. "Sweet and kind and pretty."

Chrissie squealed with laughter.

"Oh, do behave, you two," laughed Nana. "Carve the chicken for us, Roy, be a darling."

Papa Roy cut the chicken into juicy pieces, and Nana piled food onto Chrissie's plate. She gazed in awe at the feast before her. Christmas was the one time of the year that she could eat as much as she wanted—until she felt she would explode.

Papa Roy murmured grace, and they tucked in. "Merry Christmas, everyone," said Nana.

"Merry Christmas, my loves," said Papa Roy.

"Merry Christmas." Chrissie giggled, biting into a glorious floury potato.

Nana smiled at her with her head to one side, the way she often did. "And almost happy birthday to Chrissie."

The thought of her birthday suddenly reminded Chrissie of Peter with his hard eyes and his mean words. *She shouldn't even have been born.* Jonah had said it wasn't true, but she had often wondered why she didn't have a mama and papa like the other children. She loved Nana Beulah and Papa Roy, but they weren't her mother and father, were they? Tears stung her eyes, and she stared down at her plate.

"Why, Chrissie, whatever is the matter?" asked Nana.

Chrissie stared up at Nana with tears threatening in her eyes. "Nana, why don't I have a mama and a papa?" she asked.

"Peter Green said that because of that, I shouldn't have been born. He said it makes me dirty." She began to cry.

"Oh, Chrissie, darling, don't listen to that nasty little boy." Nana put a hand on her arm.

"I'll be having a word with his father," Papa Roy muttered angrily.

"There's no need of that, Roy. Our Chrissie is a strong girl." Nana smiled. "She's all right. She can handle herself, can't you, pet?" Nana kissed the top of her head. "Don't you listen to any of that rubbish, poppet. You're strong and lovely and important, and you're not dirty. You're my favorite Christmas gift, and you mustn't pay those other children any mind."

Chrissie smiled. She thought of Jonah calling her Princess Chrissie, and the thought made it even easier to push away the memory of Peter Green and his harsh words.

"I love you, Nana," she said.

Nana beamed. "We love you too, dear."

And just like that, it was once again a merry Christmas.

PART II

CHAPTER 3

Two Years Later

COLD AIR SWIRLED around Chrissie's cheeks, snatching at her steaming breath as she raced across the pond. The hiss of the skates on the ice quickened as she stretched her limbs, her scarf whipping around her shoulders.

"Hooray, Chrissie. Go. Go," cried Jonah. He stood at the end of the pond, his arms held out.

Chrissie tried to slow down, but her skates were flying on the ice, and she knew a moment of utter panic as the bank of the pond rushed up to meet her. Instead, Jonah threw his arms around her, and they both spun around, laughing. She was safe.

"You were so quick," he said admiringly. "Princess Chrissie raced the ice monsters and won."

Chrissie giggled. Even though Jonah was eleven years old, he'd told her that he'd never be too old for fairytales.

"Do you want to go again?" he asked her, eyes dancing.

Chrissie felt her smile sag as she looked up at the sun, which was slipping down the afternoon sky. "I'm sorry," she said softly. "I have to go help Nana and Papa."

"Of course. Come on. Let me take the skates off for you." Jonah took her arm, leading her across the ice to the log beside the pond where they sat down. He started to undo the laces.

"Will you tell your brother thank you for lending us his skates?" Chrissie asked.

"I already did." Jonah grinned. "Now that we can only play on Saturdays, with me working on the farm in the week and all, I just wanted to make it even more fun."

"It was very fun." Chrissie grinned. "Tell him thank you from me, too."

"I will." Jonah plucked off one of the skates and held out her boot to her. "How are your Nana and Papa doing, in any case?"

Chrissie stared out at the cold, still grey of the frozen pond.

"I think Papa's a little better," she said, "though his rheumatism doesn't like the cold at all. But Nana... she was coughing again this morning." She sucked in a frightened breath.

Jonah pulled off the other skate. "I'm sure they'll get well soon, Chrissie."

Chrissie nodded, but she wasn't so sure. Nana and Papa had been getting gradually worse for the past two years; there was a curling fear deep in the pit of her stomach that told her they never would be well again.

"Come on, Chrissie. Smile a little." Jonah grinned at her, rising to his feet. "Tell me a beautiful story about Princess Chrissie and Prince Jonah as we walk home."

Chrissie smiled. "All right, but only if you help me."

"Of course." Jonah took her hand, helping her to her feet. "Always."

BEULAH bent low over the child, even though the movement sent pangs of pain through her back and chest. She brushed some of Chrissie's beautiful soft hair out of her face and pressed her lips to the smooth, pink cheek, so shining with youth.

"Goodnight, darling," she whispered.

Fast asleep, Chrissie didn't stir, but her lashes fluttered slightly where they swept down so long and low that they nearly touched her cheek.

Beulah gazed down at the girl for a little longer. Then she blew out the candle and turned to the door. Roy stood in the doorway, holding a candlestick himself, his nightcap's pointy end dangling over one shoulder.

"She's sound asleep, the sweet lamb," Beulah whispered, stepping through the doorway.

Roy peered around the door, smiling. "Precious thing."

"Isn't she?" Beulah pulled the door shut gently. She managed to close it all the way before a spasm of coughing seized her. She doubled over, every cough tearing through her throat and setting her chest on fire.

Roy patted her back helplessly until it was over, and then Beulah's breath rattled painfully in her throat. She blinked a few times, breathing heavily, trying to catch her breath. Roy didn't ask her if she was all right. He knew, just as she did, that she would never be all right again.

As they made their way slowly downstairs to their own bedroom, Beulah clung to Roy's hand tightly. It was not death that she had feared. Why celebrate Christmas at all if she hadn't believed so fiercely, in what would come after death? No, she knew that everlasting light and peace awaited her.

It was leaving Roy and Chrissie behind that terrified her.

They slipped into their bed, groaning as old bones met the straw mattress, and Beulah pulled the covers up to her chin. She was so cold.

"Do you want another blanket, dear?" Roy asked her softly, setting the candle down on the nightstand.

"No thank you. I'll warm up in a minute." Beulah shivered a little.

Roy lay down beside her. Before he could blow out the candle, she gripped his hand under the covers. "Roy..."

"What is it, dear?"

"It's..." Beulah's eyes filled with tears. "Oh, Roy, darling, what will happen to Chrissie when we're gone?"

Roy studied her for a few moments, offering no argument. He knew the brutal logic as well as she did: they were very, very old, and Chrissie was very, very young.

"I can't bear the thought of her being all alone," Beulah cried.

"She won't be, dear," said Roy. "I'll see to that." He lay back on his pillow. "You still haven't heard from Dovie?"

"Not a word." Beulah shook her head. "It's as you said, love. She's gone."

"She's gone, but her mother isn't. Perhaps Carol could be persuaded to take an interest in the child." Roy sighed. "I'll go to see her in the morning."

"But Carol hasn't spoken to us in years, love. Not since she married that rich fellow."

"That was decades ago, Beulah." Roy kissed her cheek in a way that still made her stomach flutter after all these years. "Maybe she's had a change of heart. I'll go in the morning and see if she'll talk to me."

Beulah nestled her face back into the pillow, still breathing hard. She smiled, ignoring the pain in her chest. "Thank you, my love."

"Anything for you and Chrissie," Roy murmured, and Beulah knew with all of her heart that he meant it.

❦

ROY'S old knees ached fiercely, forcing him to pause for breath every few steps even though he dug his walking stick into the ground heavily with every stride. But he had finally reached the gates of the Brentcliff house.

Trembling with pain and exhaustion, Roy glanced back at the road at the bottom of the hill. It was the road into London, and he could see the city from here, a great black stain upon the face of the countryside with a cloud of filthy air hanging over it. He'd been lucky to be able to ride in a farmer's wagon this far; he could only hope that he'd be back down the hill in time to catch the wagon back home. There was no way these old knees, which ached so simply after climbing the hill, would bear him back to Beulah and Chrissie.

Chrissie. The thought of the child, with her huge, angelic eyes and adorable smile, spurred Roy on. He plodded up to the huge wrought-iron gate set in the high wall that surrounded the Brentcliff house. The house itself towered at the top of the hill, tall and proud, all windows and balconies and turrets. There was a huge Christmas tree on the front lawn, and bows and wreaths hung on every surface of the mansion even though it was still weeks before Christmas.

Roy was looking around for a bell when there was a great clattering of hooves. To his surprise, a carriage came rattling around the back of the house. It stopped in front of the main doors, and from this distance Roy's old eyes could just make out a lady and gentleman getting into it.

The carriage rattled toward the gate, and as it neared, Roy could finally pick out the face of the lady riding within. Powdered and rouged, it was difficult to imagine that this was the woman who had grown up out of the rosy-cheeked young girl who used to play in the field behind Roy's and Beulah's house, who used to cheerfully scrub the kitchen and feed the chickens, who used to laugh and sit on Roy's knee. Now, Carol's face was drawn and haughty, and she glared at Roy as the footman jumped down and swung the gates open.

Roy didn't give them a chance to drive away. He pushed past the footman and marched straight up to Carol's window.

"Carol, darling," he said, "it's your papa. There's something we must talk about."

Carol looked away. "I can't speak to you now, Papa. We're on our way into the city."

Roy's heart broke. The sound of his daughter's voice was so musical, so wonderful, that he longed to wrap her in his arms. Yet she would not meet his eyes.

"Darling, please. There's something you should know—about Dovie."

Carol gave him a long, hard glare. "Dovie is dead to me," she spat. "I don't want to hear her name anymore—or yours." She turned away. "Let's go."

"Carol, please." Roy cried.

He had to leap out of the way so that the carriage wheel wouldn't run him over as the horses plunged forward and clattered down the hill. And even though Roy believed he had given up hoping in his daughter many years ago, his heart still broke and bled in his chest as he plodded all the way back down the hill to the road.

※

JONAH'S blistered hands trembled on the handle of the pitchfork. It was an old thing, unbearably heavy, and its rusty head wobbled dangerously as he hauled another forkful of hay from the stack in the loft. Grunting with the effort, ignoring the pain in his hands and feet, Jonah plodded down the ladder and tossed the hay into the calves' rack.

Lowing and butting each other out of the way, the three calves hurried to the rack and began to pull hungrily at the hay. Jonah leaned over their stall partition, gazing down at them. Their coats were long and fluffy at this time of year, but they stood knee-deep in the golden straw he had spent the entire morning putting down for them, and the frigid wind howling around the corners of the barn couldn't reach them.

"I wish I was as warm as you," he told the calves.

They continued chewing on their hay and looking at him with big, brown eyes.

Jonah sighed. No wonder he was beginning to talk to calves. Farmer Green seldom came out to the barn; Peter had been sent to school in London, and so it was just Jonah and the calves in the barn.

He missed Chrissie so much.

Picking up a metal pail by the door, Jonah pushed it open and struggled into the blowing snow outside. As he plodded to the well and slowly began to lower the pail on the rope, Jonah couldn't stop thinking about her laughter or the way she always made the world brighter just by being a part of it.

"I wish you were here to tell me a story right now, Princess Chrissie," he mumbled, tugging at the rope with an effort to bring the full bucket back up from the well. At least the water down there wasn't frozen; otherwise, he would have to melt snow over a fire to water the cattle, and it would take even longer.

Even so, the water steamed with cold. When Jonah gripped the handle, it felt sticky as the cold water froze to his bare, blue fingers. Gasping with the pain in his digits, he stumbled back into the blessed warmth of the barn and tipped the pail into the calves' trough. They ignored him, continuing with their feast of hay.

Putting down the pail, Jonah brought his blue fingers to his mouth and blew on them, shivering all over. Farmer Green wasn't unkind but working for him was appalling. It never stopped, and Jonah's body hurt all over. But what else could he do? There was already barely enough to go around for all his brothers and sisters as it was. Without the few coins he earned from Farmer Green, Jonah knew his family would go hungry.

He sighed, rubbing his fingers together, and bent to pick up the pail again. The horses and cows still needed watering, too. Trudging out into the snow, Jonah closed his eyes against the driving wind, and thought of Chrissie's laughter.

And that gave him the strength to go on.

BEULAH TOOK A DEEP BREATH, even though it made her chest burn. She coughed it out as the tinker's wagon trundled to a halt outside the nice brick house in the suburb of the village just over the hill from their home.

"There y'are," said the tinker cheerfully, grinning at them. "Are you sure you'll be able to get back?"

"Aye, we will, thank you." Roy gave the tinker a penny for his trouble. "We'll catch the stagecoach; it won't cost us much if we ride on the back."

"Whatever you say, guv'nor," said the tinker, and drove away.

Beulah brushed road dust from her skirt. The journey to the next village had taken only an hour. She wasn't sure how it was possible that her body ached so relentlessly from that short ride on the tinker's wagon, and she wiped sweat from her brow despite the cold, clear day.

"Come on, love." Roy offered her his arm. "Let's go talk to Theodore."

"All right," Beulah murmured. Somewhere she found the strength to take Roy's arm, and he led her through a pretty iron gate and up to the house itself. It was a very nice house; not particularly large, but thoroughly prosperous in its way, with snow draped on its eaves and a beautiful fat wreath hanging on the door. The wreath trembled a little as Roy knocked with a big brass knocker.

The door swung open at once, with a plump woman answering it. There was a baby on her hip, and he giggled, sucking on his fist, when Beulah smiled at him.

"I don't have anything to give you," the woman said, making to close the door.

Roy stepped forward. "We're no beggars, ma'am," he said. "Mr. Wentworth is expecting us."

The woman's eyes narrowed. "Theodore," she shouted into the house. "You have visitors."

A slight, stooped man appeared in the hallway. He was balder than Beulah remembered, but he still had the same soft smile that lit up the pale eyes behind his round eyeglasses.

"Mr. and Mrs. Ellis, how good to see you," Theodore Wentworth said warmly. "Come to my study."

"Who are these people?" his wife asked sharply.

Theodore squeezed her hand feebly. "These are very old friends, my dear. Mr. and Mrs. Ellis testified in my father's case when he was just a little lad accused of stealing. They knew he hadn't done it, and they stood up for him—which kept him from being hanged."

Mrs. Wentworth's eyes narrowed. "I didn't know your father was accused of stealing."

"That was a very long time ago, my dear," said Theodore. "And all that it means is that I was inspired to become a solic-

44

itor myself, and the Ellises are our friends for life. Would you be so good as to bring us some tea?"

"Tea," huffed Mrs. Wentworth. "I have four children to feed, and the man wants tea."

She stormed away, and Theodore gave them an apologetic smile. "She's been a little irritable since the baby was born."

"He's beautiful," Beulah told him as they followed him down a long, snug hallway.

"I think so, too, but Carrie just hasn't been the same." Theodore showed them into a modest study, with a fire leaping in the hearth and a small wreath hanging from the mantelpiece. He sat down behind his desk, while Roy and Beulah took the chairs opposite his. "Now, how can I help you?" Theodore asked. "Has that landlord of yours been giving you difficulty again? I assure you, he must stay true to the terms of your agreement—I will be more than willing to write to his own solicitor again."

"Thanks to you, Theodore, our landlord is now as sweet as pie," Roy told him. "He hasn't given us a day's trouble."

"Not one." Beulah laughed. "And he hasn't made our rent more expensive in two years. You truly worked miracles for us there."

Theodore smiled. "It's good to know that I could help you. Are you well?"

Beulah and Roy exchanged a glance. Roy looked away, squeezing her hand, and Beulah took a deep breath and met Theodore's eyes. "I'm afraid not, Theodore. In fact, that is exactly why we have come to you today."

Theodore sat back in his chair. "What's the matter? Can I help?"

"I'm afraid no one can help, dear," said Beulah. "The doctor says I have cancer of the lung. Part of my youth spent in the cotton factory, you know. There's nothing to be done about it."

Roy's hand trembled as it gripped Beulah's. She squeezed it gently.

Theodore's shoulders slumped. "I'm so sorry to hear that, Mrs. Ellis."

"It's nothing to me, dear. I've had a good, long, and happy life, with only a few regrets, and that's more than most folks ever get to say." Beulah smiled. "But there's one great worry I have in life, and if you could ease it for me, it would lift a great burden from my shoulders."

"Of course. Anything," said Theodore eagerly.

Roy sat up a little straighter. "As you know, Theodore, our great-granddaughter lives with us. She's nearly eight years old now, and we've been raising her since she was just a little bairn."

"Ah, yes." Theodore looked troubled. "Do you want me to assist you in finding her mother? I'm afraid I can't think of a legal recourse to force Carol to take care of the child."

"That's not what we're asking," said Roy softly.

Theodore frowned. "Then what are you asking?"

Beulah nodded to Roy, encouraging him. The old man took a deep breath and turned to Theodore. "You're the only friend we have, Theodore," he said softly, "the only person we can ask. So you must know that we do not do this lightly."

Theodore listened, biting his bottom lip. His father had done the same thing decades ago, Beulah remembered, when he had been a frightened little boy standing trial.

"We will not be alive forever," said Roy softly. "Perhaps only a few more years. Our great-granddaughter—Chrissie—she's still so young. Someone must care for her. Please, Theodore... we beg you to consider taking her in if something should happen to us both."

"Chrissie's a good girl," Beulah added quickly. "She'd pull her weight around the house. She works hard, she's polite and kind, and she's never any trouble. She'd be very helpful to you."

"You want me to—to become the child's guardian, should you pass away?" Theodore slumped back in his chair, wide-eyed.

"It's a great thing to ask, Theodore," said Beulah, "but we have nobody else. Please. You know we don't."

Theodore opened and shut his mouth a few times, squirming visibly in his chair. "Well—I—I don't know what Carrie would say," he croaked out eventually.

Beulah's heart sank. She knew full well what Carrie would say; the harassed Mrs. Wentworth would say no, because she had no idea what the Ellises had done for Theodore's father all those years ago.

Theodore squared his shoulders. "But then again, it is not Carrie who owes you this debt," he said. "I wouldn't even be here if it wasn't for you, Mr. and Mrs. Ellis. I owe you this much—in fact, I owe you my life." He raised his chin. "I will assist you in drawing up the necessary papers so that, in the tragic event of your both passing on, Chrissie will come to stay with me."

Beulah let out a long breath she had not realized she had been holding. She pressed a hand to her heart. "Oh, Theodore, thank you. You have no idea how much peace you have brought to my heart by saying that."

Theodore tried to smile. "Don't worry, Mrs. Ellis. It will be many, many years yet before anyone has to worry for Chrissie."

She could see that he hoped so, and not only because he wished a long life for Roy and Beulah. There was real fear in the solicitor's eyes, but Beulah knew he would still make good on her promise.

And she knew, as surely as she felt the steady pain in her chest that grew every day, that Chrissie would need him far sooner than any of them hoped.

CHAPTER 4

CHRISSIE'S back and arms stung with exhaustion. She leaned back, pulling hard to get the sheet out of the tub of tepid water. Nana always said that she had to wash the laundry in hot water, but the morning was marching on, and it had taken her so very long to melt the snow even to lukewarm in the cauldron over the fire.

She tugged again, wincing at the sight of a stain on the edge of the sheet. Hot water would have washed it out, she knew. Nana would have told her that sheets should be purest white, but then again, if she could, Nana would be down here helping her get everything done—kneading the bread, stoking the fire, washing the laundry, cleaning the dishes, sweeping the floor.

Only Nana couldn't get out of bed today. She was upstairs; Papa Roy had said that she was asleep. Chrissie hoped she would feel far better when she woke up. Even if Nana couldn't pick up heavy things anymore and often needed to sit down for a rest at the kitchen table, just her presence in the kitchen made everything a little easier.

The sheet was stuck on something. The handle of the tub, perhaps. It seemed to weigh as much as the whole world, and the water dripping from it over Chrissie's hands and running across her forearms and into her dress was bitterly cold. She gasped at the chill of droplets that made it all the way up her arm and onto her ribs, and with a final despairing tug, she hauled the sheet toward her. It shot into her arms, but so did the tub. Clattering onto its side, the tub belched its contents all over the kitchen floor, icy water slopping over Chrissie's shoes.

"No. No, no, no," Chrissie cried, dropping the sheet. It fell onto the dirty floor, mud smearing it, and Chrissie gasped with shock as she gathered it into her arms and struggled to lift it back into the upturned tub. With a great struggle, she managed to turn the tub the right way up and dumped the sheet into it. The front of her dress was soaked through, and the entire kitchen floor was wet.

"Chrissie?" Papa Roy hurried into the kitchen. "What was that?"

Chrissie swallowed her tears, looking up at him. "It was an accident, Papa. I knocked it over... I... I'm so sorry." She burst into tears. "I'm so tired and I was trying to take the sheet out, but now it's all dirty again and the floor is so wet, and I feel like the world is just too big for me."

"Now, now, Chrissie." Papa sighed. "Here—get the mop and clean up as well as you can. I can't help you right now. I must go to the apothecary for more medicine for your Nana." His face was grey and lined with worry. "Why don't you take her a cup of tea before you carry on with the laundry?"

Chrissie dashed the tears away from her face, swallowing hard.

"And put on some dry clothes, pet," Papa added, relenting. "You'll catch your death like that."

"Yes, Papa, I will."

"Good girl." Papa headed outside.

Grasping the mop, Chrissie did her best to contain the worst of the spill. Her back and hands ached terribly, and she trembled all over when she hurried upstairs to change into her only other dress. It was a little too small for her, but the relief of wearing something warm and dry was glorious.

She didn't stay warm for long. Rushing outside, she scooped up pail after pail of snow, tipping it into the cauldron over the fireplace. Even after she had stoked the fire with a few sticks of wood from the pile that Papa Roy had stacked in the autumn, it seemed to take years for the snow to melt down into water that she could scoop into the kettle, and even longer for the kettle to boil.

Chrissie's eyes burned with tiredness by the time she went down the short hallway with Nana Beulah's tea on a tray. She knocked on the door, noting how badly the paint had begun to peel.

"Come in," Nana croaked.

Chrissie pushed the door open and stepped into the small room. Nana lay abed, her white hair a cloud around her face, propped up on their two pillows. There was some weak sunlight reaching into the room from the small window, and a well-worn book lay by Nana's side.

"What are you reading, Nana?" Chrissie asked, setting the mug down on the nightstand.

"Ah, thank you, dear." Nana smiled, touching the spine of the book. "It's the Good Book, my darling. I'm reading about the birth of our Savior."

"About Christmas, then," said Chrissie. She sat down on the edge of the bed, reluctant to go back out into the kitchen and deal with the pile of laundry that awaited.

"That's right." Nana sighed, sagging back against her pillows. "It was a day of such hope, my dear. A day of joy and glorious celebration... and yet it must have been a night of such cold and fear for Mary."

Chrissie nodded. She remembered, back before Nana Beulah had gotten sick, when they had owned a goat. She would never forget the goat's cries the night that she had given birth to twins. Both the goat and her kids were all right, but Chrissie had learned all about birth that night, as country children do.

"Mary was very young, you know," Nana murmured. "But she persevered, and she brought our Redeemer into this world."

"Mary was very brave," said Chrissie.

Nana smiled up at her, touching her cheek. "Just like you."

"Oh, not like me, Nana." Chrissie hung her head, thinking of how she'd wept over that wet floor. "Maybe like Princess Chrissie."

"It's a lovely game you and Jonah play," Nana murmured, "but you *are* a princess, my love. Because of Christmas, all of us are princes and princesses." She took Chrissie's hand. "Never forget it."

Chrissie wasn't sure what that meant, but she knew Nana looked tired, so she nodded. "Yes, Nana. I won't."

"That's a good girl." Nana sagged back against her pillows, her eyelids fluttering. "Chrissie, darling?"

"Yes, Nana?"

"You know that I love you, don't you?" Nana's words were a whisper on the cusp of hearing.

Chrissie took Nana's hand, holding it tightly. It was very cold. "I know that."

"Good." Nana let out a long sigh.

"I love you, too, Nana," Chrissie added. "Very, very much."

Nana's lips quirked, but she didn't say anything. She must be asleep. Chrissie slipped her hand away and tiptoed out of the wrong.

She only hoped that Nana would wake up before her tea went cold.

❦

ROY SHIVERED, the cold wind nipping sharply at the cracks of flesh that showed between his coat and his hat and gloves. He tugged at the collar, then at his sleeve. Despite the bright sunshine, unusual on Christmas Eve, the cold was still as fierce as ever. Perhaps fiercer. It seemed that winters had only grown longer and more frigid as the years went past.

Roy paused, tucking his walking stick under his arm as he rubbed his gloved hands together. The apothecary lived on the other side of the village; a quick jaunt when Roy was just a lad, but now it felt like a dreadful trek. At least, he could see his own cottage now, dusted with snow and waiting among a little row of others. He realized with a pang that his house was the only one that didn't have a wreath on the front door. With Beulah being so ill these past two weeks, ever since they had come back from visiting Theodore Wentworth, the thought of Christmas had fled from his mind.

Sighing with the pain and worry that pressed down upon his soul, Roy shuffled onward, grunting as his old bones complained. He reached his free hand into his coat pocket and felt for the two round objects in a brown paper bag inside, and a tiny smile touched his lips. There was no chance of roast chicken and potatoes for Christmas dinner this year, not with Beulah being ill. But he wouldn't let this Christmas go by completely unnoticed. Two fat, juicy oranges waited in his pocket, one for each of the two girls who made his world go around.

The thought cheered him. Chrissie would be so delighted by an orange, and perhaps it would even made Beulah feel better. He clung to that hope as he reached his home and stumbled through the unadorned door.

Chrissie had somehow cleaned up all the dirty water from the floor, poor little mite. She was busy hanging wet clothes now on the clothes-horse in front of the fireplace, her small fingers blue with cold and trembling with exhaustion. Roy felt a familiar pang of guilt for the burden of responsibility they had been forced to place on the girl's shoulders. He pulled one of the oranges out of his pocket and hid it behind his back.

"I have something for you, Chrissie dear," he said.

Chrissie's eyes lit up. "I... I thought we'd all forgotten about Christmas Eve," she whispered.

"We never forget Christmas, pet." Roy crouched down. "And Christmas is glorious no matter how hard our lives are." He lifted the orange out from behind his back and held it out to her.

"Oh, Papa." Chrissie's big eyes lit up at once, her wide smile splitting her face, tugging hard at Roy's heart. He had loved Carol, and he had loved Dovie, but it was Chrissie's smile that filled his world with light. She ran straight past the orange and into his arms, hugging him.

"Now, then," Roy grumbled, though in truth the softness of the little girl's arms around his neck was wonderful.

Chrissie stepped back, gently taking the orange. "I'll cut it into three for us all," she announced.

Roy's smile deepened. "No need for that." He produced the other orange.

"Oh, Papa, two oranges." Chrissie gasped, reverently taking the other one. She looked up at him, eyes shining. "May I show Nana?"

"Of course, you may, pet," Roy chuckled.

Chrissie stampeded down the hallway, her exhaustion forgotten in a tide of youthful exuberance. "Nana. Nana," she was shouting. "Nana, look what I have."

"Quietly, pet," Roy called after her, following her as quickly as his stiff joints would allow. "She might be sleeping. Don't wake her."

But there was no need to be concerned about waking Beulah. Roy knew it as soon as the door swung open, and he heard Chrissie's frightened gasp. He knew it even before he stepped through the doorway and looked at her grey, waxy face, her eyes closed, eternal peace upon her expression.

Beulah had fallen into a sleep from which Chrissie would not wake her.

❦

THEY BURIED Nana Beulah in the frozen earth on Christmas Day.

Chrissie clung tightly to Papa Roy's hand while the younger men dug the hole. They stood in the tiny graveyard behind the little church, and it was snowing, not the fat white flakes that Chrissie loved, but a thin tumbling of cold that made her shiver to her very bones.

She had sat in this church so often, even played in the garden outside with Jonah. Now, like everyone else, Jonah was pale and silent as they stood in a circle around the grave. Everyone wore black. Chrissie didn't have anything black to wear, so Jonah had borrowed a black dress from his sister. It was much too big, and it hung over her like a shroud.

The young men shoveled out a last forkful of black earth. "We won't get it any deeper, sir," said one of them. "It's just too frozen."

The vicar took a step nearer, peered into the hole. "It'll have to do."

It'll have to do. Nana Beulah deserved better than that, but what could anyone do? Frozen earth was frozen earth. Nana Beulah would have been upset that they were all standing outside getting cold and wet. She would have wanted everyone in the warm, with a cup of hot tea and some biscuits if there were any left.

But Nana Beulah was gone.

Tears streamed down Chrissie's cheeks. She tried her best to be brave and not sob too loudly, but she saw Jonah look at her. His mouth turned down at the corners, and he began to cry too, even though he was a boy.

"Come, Chrissie," Papa croaked.

He led her up to the grave. Chrissie didn't want to look. She'd already seen Nana in her open casket in the church, and she didn't look like Nana at all, not with her face so very still and her eyes closed, and her hands folded upon her chest. But the casket was closed when she peeped into the grave. It looked far too small to contain Nana, but it did.

Papa took a handful of the pile of dirt lying beside the grave and cast it inside. It struck the top of Nana's casket with a terrible thudding sound.

"You too, Chrissie," Papa whispered.

Chrissie didn't think she was brave enough. She reached out and gripped the handful of soil. It was bitterly cold, so cold that her fingers went numb almost at once, and she shivered. It must be so terrible, she thought, to be buried in this cold dirt. Only if Nana was right about everything she believed, then what they were burying wasn't Nana at all. She was in a glorious place of light and joy.

Chrissie sobbed. She had to hold onto that belief. It was everything, and it had been everything to Nana, too. She reached out and scattered the handful of sand into the grave, and then she turned and buried her face in Papa Roy's coat, and she sobbed until she felt her heart would burst.

There were no carolers in the village that Christmas Day.

PART III

CHAPTER 5

ONE YEAR Later

CHRISSIE RAN AS FAST as her short legs could carry her, her shoes crunching on the golden carpet of leaves underfoot. Running seemed much harder than it had been before, but she still did it, her feet aching, her back stinging as she went. She scrambled up the long slope with her heart thudding wildly in her ears, climbing the last part on her hands and knees to reach the top.

"Jonah," she gasped, squealing with delight.

He was already there waiting for her, and his eyes danced as he held something behind his back. "Hello, Chrissie."

Chrissie laughed. It felt so good to laugh; she didn't think that she had laughed once in the entire week since she had last seen Jonah. "Hello."

"I have something for you." Jonah didn't quite let his smile escape, but Chrissie could see it bubbling in his eyes.

"What is it?" she asked.

"An early Christmas present." Jonah brought his hands out from behind his back and shyly held a small object out to her.

Chrissie gasped with delight. A small, smooth river pebble lay on Jonah's palm, with a thin leather string tucked through a hole in the middle of it.

"Oh," she gasped. "It's beautiful."

"It's for you." Jonah's smile was shy.

Chrissie held out her hands, and he gently tipped the little object into them, his eyes shining. "For me?" she breathed.

"I found the stone with the hole in it at the stream when I was working for Farmer Green yesterday," said Jonah. "He gave me the bit of leather to make you a necklace."

Chrissie had never had a necklace before. It was the most magnificent thing she had ever seen. "Please help me to put it on?" she asked.

Jonah helped, tying the leather string at the back of her neck, and Chrissie admired the tiny stone where it rested on her chest. She grinned up at him. "It's so pretty. Thank you."

"I'm glad you like it." Jonah sat down on the roots of the old, gnarled oak tree that grew at the top of Farmer Green's field with a groan.

Chrissie noticed the red blisters on his hands and glanced at the field. It was mostly stubble now, but she could still see some wheat waiting for harvest in the next field. "I'd hoped your harvest would be done by now."

"So did I. Farmer Green fears it'll snow next week. We have to get *all* of this wheat in on Monday." Jonah sighed. "We feared he would want me to work today."

"But it's Sunday afternoon," Chrissie protested. "That would just be wrong."

"Some people don't care about right and wrong when it doesn't suit them." Jonah shrugged. "I'm glad Farmer Green said we could rest today. I doubt I'll be able to even lift a scythe, let alone swing it." He held up his painful hands. "My arms feel like they've been turned to stone."

"Poor, poor Jonah." Chrissie sat down beside him, sighing. "I'm sorry."

"Don't you be sorry. Things aren't easy for you this time of year either, are they?" Jonah asked.

Chrissie stared down at her own callused hands. "I don't know how to pickle things the way Nana always used to do." Tears blurred her eyes, and she blinked them back. "I'm trying, but I ruined a whole batch of cucumbers and I know we couldn't afford to lose them."

"Was Mr. Ellis angry?" Jonah asked.

"No... no. You know Papa Roy. He's not like that." Chrissie bit her lip. "I almost wish he *would* be angry, though. I wish he would be happy or afraid or *anything*. All he does is sit in his chair, and do his work, and then sit in his chair and stare at nothing. It's as though all the light went out of him after Nana died."

"I hope he still gets paid all right, for his work," said Jonah.

"They keep making his wages less and less, since he's getting so old." Chrissie sighed. "But it hardly matters because Papa doesn't eat much anymore. I wish he would. He seems so weak." She covered her face with her hands.

"Is he ill?" Jonah asked.

"The doctor came to see him, and he says there's nothing wrong, except for his sore old joints." Chrissie sighed. "I just wish I could make him better, Jonah. I want to make him better."

"I'm sorry." Jonah put an arm around her shoulders. "Let's talk of other things, though. Do you know what happened yesterday?"

"What?" Chrissie asked.

"My papa said that we could go into the pine woods in two weeks' time and cut down a Christmas tree of our very own." Jonah grinned widely. "We'll decorate it with gingerbread men and things. I want you to come and help us when you can."

"Oh, that's wonderful." Chrissie smiled. "I know it's still some weeks away, but I hope Christmas will make things better." She paused. "Even if Nana died on Christmas Eve, I hope there's still magic in it."

"There will be," said Jonah warmly. "You'll be in it."

Chrissie giggled, reaching up to hold the soft smooth stone where it rested on her chest. When she was with Jonah, it felt as though everything would be all right.

It felt as though nothing was impossible.

❦

"I'M HOME, PAPA ROY," Chrissie called, pushing the door open.

A draft howled through the cottage, coming in through the hole at the bottom of the door and whistling out of the broken windowpane in the kitchen. It stirred Papa Roy's long, unkempt hair where it straggled over his shoulders. He sat in his worn old rocking chair, not rocking, not reading, not doing anything except staring into the heart of the fire.

"Hello, pet," he grunted. His voice was a feeble thing, a grey ghost of its former self.

Chrissie went into the kitchen and propped an old cutting board against the window in a bid to block off the draft. She paused to kiss Papa on the cheek. "I'll make supper now. There's lovely fresh bread and some butter from the milkmaid. I think the bread is almost still warm. Doesn't that sound nice?"

Papa nodded but said nothing. Chrissie stared at him for a few moments. She wanted to scream, to shake him, to force him to his feet. But the old man simply stared into the flames, a wasted skeleton of the giant he had once been.

She sighed and took the bread from the bread bin, then cut it slowly, trying to avoid hurting her fingers—she had cut and burned herself so often in the past eleven months since Nana had died. But it didn't matter now. What mattered was the butter, which was gloriously golden. Surely it would be enough to tempt Papa's appetite.

She set the slice of buttered bread on a plate and held it out to him where he sat by the fire. "Here, Papa. Isn't that lovely? I'm making tea, too. Dig in—there's plenty if you want some more."

Papa blinked down at his plate, taking it almost by reflex. "Thank you," he mumbled.

Chrissie sat down near him, devouring the fresh bread in hungry gulps. But Papa barely picked at a corner of it. He kept staring into the flames.

She wished she knew what he was seeing in them. She inched a little closer, putting a hand on his knee. "Papa, please eat," she whispered. "You'll feel better."

Papa Roy stared at her. "Don't cry, Chrissie," he murmured. "Please don't cry."

Chrissie swallowed, fighting back her tears. "I don't know what I'm doing wrong. I don't know why you won't eat," she cried.

Papa Roy's eyes widened. "Chrissie, pet, no." He set the plate down on the low table by the fireplace and held out his arms.

Chrissie fled into his embrace, tucking her body into a lap that was more bone than flesh. Not wincing at her sudden weight, Papa gathered her softly in his arms, kissing her forehead and her tangled hair. "You've never done anything wrong," he whispered. "You're my little girl, my love, the one thing that has been worthwhile these past few years, and I love you very much."

Chrissie clung to him. "I love you, Papa. And I need you."

Papa let out a long, soft sigh. "You're all right, Chrissie dear. You'll be all right."

"I will, because you're here," said Chrissie.

Papa Roy didn't answer. He went back to staring into the flames, and he didn't touch another bite of his supper. Chrissie ate both slices in the end, her hunger overruling her good manners, and tried to get Papa to wash and go to bed.

"It's a little cold in that room," Papa murmured. "I'll just sit by the fire a little longer. You go to bed, pet. You have laundry to do tomorrow—you need your rest."

It was true, so Chrissie cleaned the dishes and did as she was told. At the steps to her attic bedroom, she paused, looking at Papa where he sat staring into the flames. His skin was stretched tightly over his skull, but there was nothing skeletal about the sorrow in his eyes.

"Papa?" she said.

He looked up. "Yes, Chrissie?"

"Goodnight."

Papa Roy smiled, not a lot, but enough that his eyes shone. "Goodnight, pet."

She returned his smile and went up to bed. But when she woke in the night and saw that Papa's bedroom door still stood wide open, and rushed down to the kitchen to find him, there was no smiling. For Papa Roy was still and stiff in his chair, dead of a broken heart.

IT WAS STRANGE, after all this time with just her and Papa, to be in a kitchen that was a wild hubbub of noise and light and chaos.

Chrissie stared down into her bowl of porridge as the Costigan children bounced around the big room. There were five of them, including Jonah, and all but one were younger than he. Jonah himself was chewing a crust of bread.

It seemed impossible that, this time yesterday, Chrissie had been sitting in her own kitchen, eating buttered bread with Papa Roy. Now Papa Roy was gone. He would be buried tomorrow, right beside Nana Beulah. Chrissie knew they would be happy together again, that Papa Roy's broken heart would heal.

Only now she was left with the burden of her own broken heart.

"Come on, Chrissie, dear." Mrs. Costigan patted her on the top of the head. "You've not eaten a thing since you came running from your great-grandpapa's house in the middle of the night. You need to keep your strength up."

Chrissie picked up her spoon and prodded the porridge with it. She liked porridge, usually. But the thought of putting food into her mouth right now made her guts twist. Strength? She had none; her fingers felt numb and stupid.

"Eat as you're told, child," Mr. Costigan barked from the head of the table. "We've taken you in and fed you out of the goodness of our hearts. Don't let me catch you being ungrateful."

"Leave her alone, Patrick," Mrs. Costigan shot back. "Can't you see the poor lamb is grieving?"

Mr. Costigan grumbled into his bread and cheese, and Chrissie spooned up a mouthful of the porridge and swallowed it with a mighty effort. Her eyes met Jonah's over the table, and he tried to smile at her, but there were tears in his eyes. She looked away. She couldn't cry more, not today, not with Mr. Costigan glaring at her like that.

"Where's that letter, Patrick?" Mrs. Costigan asked.

Mr. Costigan glared up at her. "What letter?"

"The one that dear old Roy gave you, about a year ago now. Before Beulah passed on, God rest her sweet soul," said Mrs. Costigan.

"Oh." Mr. Costigan sat back, eyes widening. "I'd forgotten all about that."

"What letter is it, Mr. Costigan?" Chrissie asked as politely as she could.

Mr. Costigan glared at her, then got up and stomped out of the small kitchen of their cottage.

Mrs. Costigan put a hand on her shoulder. "Your great-grand-papa left it with us, dear, and said we were to read it if anything ever happened to him and your great-granny."

"What's in it?" Chrissie asked.

"I don't know, dear. But whatever it is, I'm sure it'll tell us about the arrangements they made for you."

Chrissie's heart froze in her chest. Her spoon clattered back into her bowl. "Arrangements? I—I thought I'd get to stay with you."

Mrs. Costigan lowered her head. "We have so many mouths to feed," she murmured.

Chrissie felt suddenly as though she was standing at the edge of a cliff. She shrank back in her chair, staring at Jonah. He had gone very pale.

Mr. Costigan came stomping back into the kitchen and flopped down in his chair, holding a little envelope. Chrissie saw Nana Beulah's writing on it; soft, flowing writing it was, too. She read the words just like Nana had taught her. *Jonah Costigan Senior*, it read. *In the event of our deaths.*

Death. The word haunted her.

"You read it, Mother," said Mr. Costigan.

Mrs. Costigan squeezed Chrissie's shoulder and took the letter. She cleared her throat but didn't read aloud. Chrissie still saw how her eyes widened as she read, and a terrible fear clawed at her insides.

"Oh, thank heaven," Mrs. Costigan gasped.

"What is it?" Chrissie asked. "What is it? Am I staying with you? Oh, please say that I may stay with you."

"Let her stay with us, Mama," said Jonah.

"No... no, I'm afraid not, my dear." Mrs. Costigan sat down, pressing a hand to her heart. "You know we don't have room for another... or money. But don't worry, Chrissie dear. You're going to be just fine." She smiled widely. "Everything is going to be all right."

"Why?" Chrissie asked. "How?"

"Your sweet great-grandparents made arrangements to be sure that you would be all right once they were gone," said Mrs. Costigan. "In fact, you're going to live with a very nice man in the next village. His name is Theodore Wentworth, and he's a solicitor. You're going up in the world, dear. You'll get an education and a respectable position in life."

Chrissie covered her face with her hands and sobbed. She didn't know what a solicitor was or what a respectable position in life was supposed to be, but she did hear two words: *next village.* She was leaving her home behind.

And she'd be was forced to leave Jonah behind, the only friend she had left.

"Don't cry, Chrissie." Mrs. Costigan squeezed her hand. "No, don't cry. This is good. This is wonderful for you."

"I don't want to go," Chrissie sobbed. "Don't make me go."

"Stop your racket, child," barked Mr. Costigan.

But Jonah, as usual, was the only one who could console her. He leaned over the table and patted her shoulder. "It's all right, Chrissie. We'll get Mr. Wentworth to bring you here to visit sometimes."

Chrissie's sobs slowed. She sank back in her chair. "We will?"

"Of course, we can, dear," said Mrs. Costigan. "Of course, we can."

And even though Mrs. Costigan said it in that voice that you use for little children when you tell them something just to make yourself feel better, Chrissie had no choice but to believe her.

CHAPTER 6

MR. WENTWORTH'S house was very, very big, and its windows frowned down at Chrissie like angry eyes. She swallowed hard, staring up at it. "It's so big," she whispered.

"It's only big compared to our little cottages, dear," said Mrs. Costigan. She held Chrissie by the hand as she led her up to the iron gate at the front of the garden. "But it's lovely, isn't it? Look at that lovely big garden, Chrissie. You'll have the most wonderful time here."

The garden was far smaller than Farmer Green's field where Chrissie and Jonah always played. She looked over at him. He'd insisted on walking with them, and his eyes were scared, too.

Mrs. Costigan swung the gate open, and Chrissie stumbled to a halt. She knew that if she stepped through that gate, it would close behind her, and that would be the end of her life as she had known it. Nana and Papa were gone, and soon Jonah would be gone too. It would just be Chrissie all alone with Theodore Wentworth, whoever he was.

"I don't want to go," she whispered.

Mrs. Costigan crouched down in front of her, clutching her hands. "We talked about this, dear. You know you have to. Making a fuss won't make that any better, will it?"

Jonah took her hand in his own and squeezed it. "You're a brave princess, Chrissie," he said softly. "My Princess Chrissie. And you're going to be all right."

Chrissie stared at him with watering eyes. Somehow, when he said it, it was almost possible to believe. She took a deep breath, squaring her narrow shoulders. "All right," she whispered. "And Mr. Wentworth will bring me to visit you. So I'll see you soon."

"Soon," said Jonah, smiling.

"I'm sure he will, dear," said Mrs. Costigan absently.

They walked down the garden path and Mr. Costigan knocked on the door with a big brass knocker. When it swung open, a thin man stood there, looking down at them with big soft eyes. Chrissie stared at him. He didn't seem very frightening, at least.

"Can I help you?" the man asked politely.

"Are you Theodore Wentworth?" Mrs. Costigan asked.

He nodded, and Mrs. Costigan held out the letter. "I've been given instructions to bring this little girl to you," she said.

Mr. Wentworth's eyes widened. He took the letter, unfolding it quickly, and all the blood drained out of his face.

"Mr. Wentworth?" Mrs. Costigan prompted.

He cleared his throat, his eyes darting to Chrissie. "Are they both—dead?"

"I'm afraid so, sir," said Mrs. Costigan. "We buried poor Roy just yesterday."

Mr. Wentworth rubbed the back of his neck. "Oh... this is a bad time. This is..." He stared at Chrissie, then at the letter. "But a promise is a promise." He straightened. "Very well. You must be—" He checked the letter. "Christmas Ellis."

"Nobody calls me Christmas, sir," said Chrissie. "My name is Chrissie."

"That'll do, I suppose." Mr. Wentworth sighed, glancing at the small canvas bag in her hand. "Is that all you've brought?"

"Yes, sir," said Chrissie.

Mr. Wentworth grunted. "Come inside then, child." He stepped back, holding the door open.

Chrissie stared at Jonah, who smiled at her. *Princess Chrissie*, he mouthed.

It was those words alone that gave Chrissie the courage to square her shoulders and walk into the big, scary house.

❧

THEODORE PRACTICALLY TIPTOED into the dining room. It was impossible, these days, to tell what mood Beatrice would be in when he came down for dinner; although lately it was becoming a surer and surer bet that it would be a bad one.

The housemaid was just setting the last dish of food on the table. She gave him a wide-eyed look, and he noticed that the sleeve of her black-and-white dress was patched. Then she scurried off.

"Good evening, my dear," he ventured, turning his attention to the woman sitting at the table.

Beatrice had been so pretty once. It saddened him that worry had worn such deep lines in her increasingly pale face. She fixed him with baleful eyes, watching as he took his seat and tried to smile at her.

"Good?" she demanded. "*Good?* How can it be a *good* evening when you brought another child into the house without even speaking to me about it?"

Theodore stared down at his plate, his stomach feeling hollow. It had been five long months since little Chrissie had first come to their home, and still Beatrice would never let him forget, even for a moment, what he had hidden from her.

He stared outside at the falling snow. "It's nearly Christmas, my dear," he murmured. "Can't we leave it for just one night?"

"Yes, Theodore, it's nearly Christmas, and your four children barely have a single present because you decided that it was more important to honor an arbitrary promise to some old people than to care for your own family," Beatrice shrieked.

Theodore flinched. He started to help himself to the liver and potatoes that the servants had prepared, noting with sorrow that the potatoes were even less buttery than they had been last week.

"You know what the Ellises did for my father," he murmured.

"I also know what you did to *me*." Beatrice's eyes narrowed. "Why didn't you say anything, Theodore? Why didn't you even tell me?"

Theodore let out a long sigh and stared down at his plate. There would be no question of saying table grace tonight; Beatrice wouldn't give him even that brief respite. "Because I knew you would say no," he said sharply. "I knew you would never agree."

"And with good reason," Beatrice shrieked. "Look at what you've done, Theodore. We already have four children—*four*. And since you won't dare to charge the proper rates for your services, we have no money, either. I don't even have a house-keeper. We don't even have a carriage." She covered her face with her hands. "We're ruined. *Ruined.*" With that, she began to sob.

Theodore stared at her helplessly. He had thought, back then, that he was marrying well, and everyone had been so proud of him for marrying such a well-bred woman. But the more he tried to help the villagers who were so desperate for legal assistance, the more Beatrice hated him. He wished he had married bonny little Nellie Smith instead, even if she was only a farmer's daughter.

"Beatrice, my dear..." he began.

"I told you to find a home for that child, Theodore," said Beatrice bitterly. "And don't think I don't know that you haven't even been trying."

"I have been trying," Theodore protested.

Beatrice tossed her head. "You had the perfect opportunity the other day when that old man from the farm down the road told you how he was looking for more help on the farm."

Theodore stared at her. "Giving Chrissie to him would condemn her to a life of slave labor, Beatrice."

Beatrice's eyes were cold and hard. "I don't care," she said. "You must think me cruel, but in truth, I'm thinking of our children. *Your* children, Theodore. They'll starve like this. They'll grow up neglected."

Theodore dropped his eyes to his plate. He knew, right this very second, that despite his seemingly meager wages his four children and Chrissie alike were having a plentiful dinner of liver and mash. Perhaps not the most sumptuous dinner, but they would never go to bed hungry, or want for clothes or books.

"You're ruining us, Theodore." Beatrice wailed again.

He stared at her, at her shaking hands and reddened eyes, and wondered if her nerves could last. She seemed as though she would fly apart into a billion pieces at any minute. And then what of the children?

He had no choice. He lowered his head. "Very well. I'll find a home for the girl."

"And do it before Christmas, too," barked Beatrice. "Then at least our children might have a good dinner on Christmas Day."

Theodore shoveled a forkful of potatoes into his mouth, but they tasted like they were made of sand.

❧

THE ONLY GOOD thing about the Wentworth house, even after all this time, was that Chrissie had brothers and sisters at last.

She was not allowed, of course, to call them her brothers and sisters—not when people were around. In fact, she was not even allowed to sit by them at church. Instead, she had to sit all on her own at the end of a pew where the widows sat, like a little orphan, because Mrs. Wentworth didn't want her to be seen with the family.

But in her heart, at least, Chrissie had decided that the four Wentworth children were the first siblings she had ever known—the siblings she'd only ever wished for.

She sat cross-legged on the nursery hearth with the little baby, swinging a rattle in front of his eyes. The baby was not yet two years old, and he stretched chubby fists toward the rattle, his big blue eyes utterly entranced.

"Get it, Timmy." Chrissie giggled. "Catch it."

Timmy made a grab for it with his fat baby hands and missed. He squealed with frustration, revealing his six baby teeth, and tried again. This time, Chrissie allowed him to grip the smooth wooden object, and he let out a coo of delight, shaking it up and down with all of his might.

"Would you stop that racket?" Annabelle demanded. "I'm trying to read."

Annabelle was Chrissie's big sister, and she was never not reading. She lay on her side on her bed, curled around one of the enormous books she always had.

"What are you reading?" Chrissie asked as Timmy started to chew contentedly on the rattle.

"You wouldn't understand," Annabelle sniffed.

Chrissie got up and went over to Annabelle's bed, leaning her arms on it and propping her chin on them. "Maybe I could, if you showed me."

Annabelle glared at her.

"Of course, she could, Anna," laughed Gregory softly. Gregory was her favorite sibling, although that was something she kept to herself; a brother just a year older than her, with a soft laugh that always seemed to make people smile.

It made Annabelle smile right now. "Well, all right," she grumbled, patting the bed beside her. "Get up and I'll read to you."

"Hooray," squealed a small voice from beside the toy box in the corner of the room. Chrissie's little sister, Tammy, got to her feet and toddled over as fast as she could, her big eyes wide. "Anna read."

"I won't read a thing if you don't all shut up," Annabelle warned.

Chrissie lifted Tammy onto the bed beside her, and they curled up in a heap, waiting expectantly. Even Gregory put down the piece of wood he was whittling.

"Oh, don't look at me like that," Annabelle grumbled. She lifted the book and began to read. "*An ancient English Cathedral Tower? How can the ancient English Cathedral tower be here.*"

There was a soft sound, a clearing of the throat, and all the children looked up. Tammy let out a squeal of purest joy. "Papa. Papa!" She launched off the bed and ran to the nursery door with her little arms outstretched.

Mr. Wentworth, who insisted that Chrissie call him Theodore, crouched down and scooped her little sister into his arms, showering her with kisses. Tammy shrieked with joy.

"Now what are you all doing here?" Theodore asked, putting Tammy onto the ground and bending down to tickle Timmy's cheeks.

"Annabelle's reading to us, Theodore." Chrissie jumped off the bed and ran to him, plucking at his sleeve. "Won't you sit with us? It's a good book, I think."

"You've heard only two sentences," scoffed Annabelle. "It's a bit early for judgment, I think."

"Oh, Annabelle," laughed Theodore. "You precocious poppet." He patted the top of her head and smiled at Gregory.

"Have you come to take us to the park, Papa?" Gregory asked.

"Not today, my boy. Actually, I need to speak with Chrissie." Theodore held out a hand to her. "Come, pet. Let's talk."

"Talk?" Chrissie pressed her hands into the soft folds of her lovely blue linen dress, staring at him. "What do we need to talk about?"

Theodore's face wobbled in a way that made Chrissie's stomach clench. "Just come with me, pet. It's all right." He held out his hand even further.

Chrissie looked into Theodore's soft eyes and was certain she could trust him. Her shoulders relaxed a little, and she reached out and took his hand.

"You mustn't forget to come tuck us in later, Papa," said Tammy.

"Of course, he won't forget. He and Chrissie will be back in a minute," said Annabelle.

Theodore's smile slipped again. "Yes, of course we will," he croaked.

He turned and led Chrissie out of the nursery, down the stairs and into the hall. Then he helped her into her coat, buttoning all the buttons tightly, and wrapped a scarf around her neck and put on her hat.

"It's not that cold outside, Theodore," she protested.

Theodore gave her a shaky smile. "I think it's going to turn for the worse. Let's go."

They headed out of the front door on foot and down the street. Chrissie sweated in her thick coat; it was an unseason-

86

ably sunny day, considering that it was close to Christmas. She kept a steady hold on Theodore's hand, tugging at her scarf to get a little breeze to her skin.

"What did you want to talk about, Theodore?" she asked.

"In a minute," he said. "Just a minute."

They went down the street and into the market square of the village, and Chrissie admired the wreaths that hung from every doorway, the candles in all the windows. A group of carolers went from shop to shop, singing "O Holy Night." Chrissie closed her eyes, listening to the song. "This one's my favorite," she said.

"It's a beautiful one," Theodore agreed.

He led her to the bakery, where he bought two big, fat, warm hot cross buns wrapped in brown paper. "Take these," he told her.

She held the brown paper. "We'll break them in pieces and share them with my brothers and sisters." She could almost taste their sweet warmth.

Theodore said nothing. Instead, he led her across the square to a stand near the back, where a stagecoach was waiting. They were busy changing horses, one sweaty, foaming team being led away while another was harnessed.

"Are we going to ride the stagecoach?" Chrissie asked, with a gasp of excitement. She had never been in a coach before.

Only on the back of Farmer Green's hay wagon from time to time. What a wonderful treat.

"Yes, we are," said Theodore.

He bought a ticket at the stand and led Chrissie up to the coach as the horses were harnessed.

"Where are we going?" Chrissie asked.

"You'll see in a minute," said Theodore.

She tugged at his hand with excitement as the passengers started to get in. At last, Theodore lifted her into the seat, straightened out her coat and scarf, and made sure she had a good grip on the bag of buns in her hand.

"Will we be back in time for dinner?" Chrissie asked.

Theodore looked her in the eye then for the first time since they had left the house, and she saw tears in them. They frightened her. The last time she'd seen a man cry was when Papa Roy had to bury Nana Beulah.

"Theodore?" she croaked out, gripped by a sudden terror.

"I'm sorry, Chrissie," he whispered.

Chrissie grabbed his sleeve. "Let's go home. I want to go home."

"I'm sorry. You can't." Theodore plucked his arm away. "You're going to live with nice people in London."

Chrissie felt as though she was falling into an abyss. How was this happening?

"Why?" she burst out. "I live with you now. With you and Timmy and Gregory and Annabelle and Tammy." Tears coursed down her cheeks. "I want to go home."

"I'm sorry, Chrissie. I'm sorry. We can't go home." Theodore's voice cracked. "I'm sorry."

"Take me home. Please. I want to go back to Nana and Papa's cottage, then," she sobbed. "I want to go back to Jonah." The sound of his name knifed through her heart. He had never come to see her; she had asked Theodore so many times to take her back, but he never had. "Take me back to the Costigans. Take me to Jonah."

"They're going to take good care of you. You're going to love the city," said Theodore, but he was almost crying now. "You'll be all right, Chrissie. You'll be just fine."

"No. No. NO," Chrissie screamed. "Please. Theodore, please."

But he shoved her into her seat and slammed the door, and then the coach was racing forward. Chrissie sobbed, threw herself against the window as they sped down the street, faster than she'd ever gone in her life. She caught a last glimpse of Theodore, his slender frame stooped, watching her go.

And then they left the village and everything she knew far, far behind.

CHAPTER 7

BEING in a coach was nowhere close to what Chrissie had expected.

There were so many people crammed into the coach that Chrissie found herself squeezed into the corner of her seat. The fat man beside her took up most of the space, and his elbow kept jabbing into her ribs or shoulder when he moved. No one even looked at her as she cried softly, tears spilling down her cheeks. Only a skinny little boy sitting on his mother's lap across from her kept glancing at the packet of hot cross buns on her lap. She wanted to share them, but the mother looked so angry and cold that she was too afraid. So she tucked them into the big pocket of her coat instead.

She wondered what she had done wrong for Theodore to send her away like this. Papa Roy had told her, not long before he died, that her mother had run away right after she was born. Even her grandmother didn't want her. Papa Roy hadn't said it like this, of course. He had said that her mother, Dovie, and her grandmother, Carol, were both fools not to love her, and then he'd tickled her until she'd laughed and squealed with joy. But maybe there was something wrong with her even when she was born. Maybe Papa and Nana had only loved her because nobody else did. Because they had the biggest hearts in the whole wide world.

It was no wonder Theodore didn't want her, then.

The countryside slipped away, replaced with ever-thickening buildings, ever-narrowing streets. These streets weren't lined with snow; instead, yellow-grey slush lay in the gutters, and even the snow dusting the rooftops seemed grimy compared to the perfect white of the countryside. There were no Christmas decorations here. It was as though Christmas barely existed in these streets. Perhaps that was because there were no homes here; instead, the buildings were all huge and ugly, some of them belching smoke and steam into the air, adding to the dismal grey smog that hung over everything.

The coach rattled to a halt at a stand on a street corner. No one got out, but the driver yanked the door open. "Are you Christmas Ellis?" he demanded.

Chrissie nodded silently.

"This is your stop. Get out," he ordered.

Chrissie scrambled out of the coach. "Sir, please—" But the driver had already walked away to help with harnessing the fresh team.

Chrissie didn't know what to do. She stood on the corner, staring at the big, ugly buildings, their shapes all stern and square, their windows very small, peering down at her like eyes narrowed in disapproval. The people hurrying along the sidewalks here were all so raggedy, with bare flesh showing at the toes of their shoes, their eyes yellowed and baleful as they barely glanced at Chrissie before shuffling onward. She wondered what time it was but could hear no church bells. Only a dreadful cacophony from within the buildings—factories, she guessed: clattering, metallic clanging, the growl of steam engines. They sounded a little like the train that passed by Theodore's house every now and then.

She thought of her warm bed in Theodore's house and of Tammy's little body curled up beside her when she had nightmare, and she began to cry.

"Stop that fuss, child," barked a voice. "You're Christmas Ellis, aren't you?"

So many strangers here, people who had to ask her name, where in her old village everyone had known her ever since she was a baby. This latest stranger was a scrawny man with protruding front teeth and big yellowish eyes that seemed to bulge from their sockets as they stared at her.

"Yes, sir," she quavered. "That's my name."

"You're coming with me." He held out a hand.

Chrissie backed away. "Sir, who are you?"

"I'm Bertram Jones. You're coming to stay with me. Theodore Wentworth arranged it."

Chrissie blinked up at him, a pang of hope running through her. "Are you my new papa, sir?"

"Whatever you like, child," said Bertram. "Now come with me."

He took her hand in a hard, callused claw, and led her even deeper among the factories and warehouses that growled and rumbled like stalking monsters around her. She stuck very close to Bertram, avoiding the men who sat on street corners and looked at her with crazy eyes that seemed to be half-in and half-out of this world.

At length, they reached a squat building, a little smaller than the others, that spat a constant stream of smoke and steam from its ceiling. Bertram paused in front of it, a proud smile crossing his face. "This is our factory. You'll be working here."

"What do you make, sir?" asked Chrissie. She was used to work; she'd been doing chores all her life. She supposed that the Jones children simply had their chores in this factory.

"Cotton fabric. You'll learn in the morning." Bertram jerked at her arm, leading her across a grimy street and up to the building directly across from the factory. It had many stories and rows of dirty square windows, its bare bricks dull and dirty in the fading light. When Bertram led her inside, she could hear a quiet hubbub of voices coming from all around her. It felt as though this building alone perhaps contained more people than the entire village where she had grown up.

They climbed three flights of dirty stairs, Chrissie doing her best to avoid the dark stains on every second step. At last, Bertram pushed open a door and led her into a set of rooms. The first room was quite nice, with a warm carpet and a fire crackling in the hearth, and two armchairs set facing the fire.

"The new girl's here, Chloe," said Bertram.

A woman rose from one of the armchairs. She was as plump as Bertram was scrawny, with a pug nose and hard grey eyes. They raked Chrissie. "Lovely. She looks good and healthy. And her clothes will last a while, too. Saves us having to replace them."

"Hello," said Chrissie shyly.

Chloe ignored her. "Send her to bed. She doesn't need any supper."

Somehow Chloe must have known about the buns in Chrissie's pocket. Bertram took her down a cozy hallway, then through a door into a large, cold, bare room. There was nothing on the floor here, which was made of splintery floorboards, and there were no curtains on the window. Eight sleeping pallets lined the walls, four on each side, each covered with a couple of thin blankets. There were no pillows. Chrissie gasped at the sight of all the children in the room: seven others, mostly girls, except for a surly older boy who sat on the pallet in the back corner with his arms folded. One of them coughed. No one looked at Chrissie twice.

"There's your bed." Bertram shoved her toward the pallet nearest the door. "You'll come to work with the others in the morning."

He slammed the door shut, leaving Chrissie in the dark room, lit only by the fading light in the window. She took a deep breath. "Hello," she said softly. "I'm Chrissie."

No one answered.

Chrissie reached into her pocket and pullet out the brown paper bag. She removed one of the buns—it was cold and hard now—and held it out. "Does anyone want a hot cross bun?"

Immediately, every pair of eyes was upon her. One of the smaller girls—perhaps a year or two older than Chrissie—started forward, then sank back onto her pallet. A big girl rose from a pallet near the back, opposite the boy's, and strode over to Chrissie.

"Give me that." She snatched it from Chrissie's hand and began to tear off chunks of it with her teeth.

Chrissie thought of giving her the other bun, too, but hunger gnawed at her stomach. She tucked the bag into her pocket before anyone could see that there was a bun in it.

"I'm Christmas," she said softly. "But everyone calls me Chrissie."

"I'm Jane," said the big girl, "and you'll do as I please. Now go to bed."

"Yes, Jane." Chrissie went over to her pallet and pulled aside one blanket. She lay down on the other, but it was hard and scratchy and dusty, and the pallet was like lying on bare wood. She pulled the thin blanket over her and lay looking up at the mouldy ceiling; chinks of light showed through the wood.

She wished she was in her bed in the attic of Nana and Papa's cottage, listening to them talking softly on the floor below. She wished she was stretched out on a bed of autumn leaves under the old oak tree at the top of Farmer Green's field, listening to Jonah telling her another story about Princess Chrissie. She even wished she was in her warm, soft bed in the Wentworth nursery, listening to her siblings snoring.

Instead, she listened to the clacking of the factories around her and the many strangers' voices in the building, and to Bertram and Chloe arguing loudly in the next room. And it took a very long time for sleep to find her.

IT WAS CHRISTMAS DAY, but that didn't matter to the Joneses.

The blisters on Chrissie's hands had turned into calluses, and the days had blurred together with exhaustion since she had come to London. It could have been a week; perhaps a little more. She tried to remember as she crawled beneath the cotton mule, a giant, spinning, terrifying thing that moved to and fro on thin wheels that ran on tracks. She had never heard anything as loud in her life as that cotton mule, not even thunder in the rare summer storms that rolled over the hills of her old village. The mule rumbled constantly, and every time its wheels moved, they let out a terrible, piercing shriek that tore Chrissie's ears. As a result, there was a constant buzzing in them, even when she tried to sleep.

She clutched a brush and scoop in her hands as she shuffled across the floor on her hands and knees. Over her head, hundreds of cotton threads stretched and spun. The floor was grimy with dust and oil and scraps of cotton, and Chrissie worked quickly, sweeping them into the scoop.

The tone of the mule's noises changed as it let out a great snarling roar. Chrissie gasped. She flung herself backwards, away from the wheels, and cowered against the floor between two of the tracks. The mule hissed toward her on its wheels, shrieking. She pressed her cheek to the floor, shaking with fear, as the body of the mule passed directly over her. A snag of her hair caught on it and ripped out of her skull with a sting of pain. She bit back her cry, clinging to her brush and scoop, and waited for the mule to be gone before she scrambled to her feet and dashed out of its range, rubbing the back of her head.

Suzie, the second-to-youngest of the girls, glanced at Chrissie as she carefully began to sort out the contents of the scoop—dirt into a waiting sack of garbage, bits of cotton into another sack to be spun later. Suzie worked as a piecer, fixing any bits of cotton that broke while the mule was spinning them. Catching her eye, Chrissie smiled at her.

"Do you think we'll get something nice for Christmas supper?" she asked.

Suzie quickly looked away. "We're not supposed to talk while we're working."

It was true. Chrissie stared out of one of the small, narrow windows, coughing a little on the cotton dust that hung in the air and pervaded everything. She remembered Nana Beulah saying to her doctor one time that she would never have gotten so sick if she hadn't worked in a cotton mill when she was younger. Would Chrissie die from this one day, too?

The window just looked onto a grey and silent street. No carollers. No decorations. She glanced up at the big clock on the wall instead. It was a quarter to eight; almost time for supper and bed.

"You. Christmas," shouted Bertram's voice. "What are you doing, just standing there?" He appeared around a corner, glaring at her.

"Sorry, sir." Chrissie ducked her head, took a deep breath, and got back on her hands and knees, crawling beneath the mule.

She had time for two more passes under the moving mule before the bell finally rang and the eight children trooped across the street from the factory to the building where they lived. They were offered the chance to wash their hands and faces in a tub of cold water, which stung Chrissie's skin as she splashed it on her face, desperate to be rid of the grime that packed onto her skin during her fourteen-hour day. She allowed herself a pang of excitement as the children went through to their room, where Chloe served their meals every night. Perhaps there would be something a little special tonight. Even if it was only a piece of chicken or maybe a quarter of an orange. She missed the taste of oranges so much.

Instead, Chloe didn't give them so much as a smile. Supper was watery beef soup, which Chloe ladled into their bowls expressionlessly. Just two scoops per child, barely enough. Chrissie's arms and legs had already grown bony.

When Chloe was gone, the room was filled with hungry slurping. Chrissie sat cross-legged on her pallet, staring into the bowl. It was the most miserable Christmas supper she could remember.

She looked over at Suzie, trying to smile. "Merry Christmas."

Suzie glared at her. "What are you talking about?" She slurped up some soup. "There is nothing merry here."

Chrissie's shoulders sagged.

"Shut up, all of you," barked Jane. "I've had enough noise for one day."

Silence fell. Chrissie finished her meal, washed her bowl in a tub with a rag and some tepid water, and set it on the table just as Chloe always ordered. She crawled into bed and stared up at the ceiling. Somewhere, a burst of laughter came from one of the rooms; she wished she could laugh now.

She squeezed her eyes tightly shut and gripped the smooth river stone hanging on its leather string around her neck. In her heart, she prayed softly, just like Nana had always taught her. *Dear God, please be with Nana and Papa and give them a very happy Christmas in heaven. Give them a lovely roast goose to eat, with plum pudding and baked potatoes and gravy and carrots and fruit cake. Give them a beautiful Christmas tree and lots and lots of presents from all their friends in heaven. And please, God, be with Jonah too, and let him have a nice Christmas, and keep him safe. Please let me see him again one day.* She blinked at the tears that trickled down her cheeks. *Please help me to be Princess Chrissie, if it was true what Nana Beulah said—that I'm a princess in Your eyes.*

In the nasty, smelly, cold and grimy tenement, she had never felt further from being a princess of any kind. She whispered her amen, pulled her blanket over her head, and tried her best to sleep.

CHRISSIE SCRAMBLED out from under the mule, narrowly missing one of the big metal wheels. She crouched down by the two bags in the back of the room and emptied her scoop quickly, sorting the material with brisk, efficient movements.

When she straightened up, she felt a little pang of pride, the way she used to do when she looked at the cottage kitchen all cleaned or took a loaf of bread from the oven freshly baked. Right now, the floor beneath the mule was sparkling with cleanliness. She smiled to herself. Surely Bertram and Chloe would soon notice.

There was a soft *twang* sound. Chrissie spotted a broken thread among the hundreds of fine white lines running across the mule. She glanced around for Suzie, but the girl was standing several yards away on the other end of the mule, struggling to piece together another broken thread.

Setting down her brush and scoop, Chrissie moved quickly. She dashed across to the broken thread, gripping it in both hands, and tied it with a single brisk movement—the same movement Nana had taught her when she showed her how to sew.

"What are you doing?" Bertram's voice boomed.

Chrissie whipped around. She sucked in a nervous breath, smiling up at him. "Sir, I was just piecing this thread, because it was broken, and Suzie was busy."

Bertram gave her a long look. Chrissie entangled her fingers in front of her, her heart pounding. Maybe he'd be proud of her now. Maybe that would change the way he looked at her.

It did, a little, but there was still no love in his eyes—only approval. He nodded. "The floor looks good, too. And you've done this before."

"A few times, sir. I just want to help," she added quickly. "Suzie's so very busy, and it's a big mule. I thought she might need a little help."

"She does." Bertram raised his head. "Suzie. Come here."

The other girl slouched over to him, a discontented twist to her mouth. "Yes?"

Bertram turned to Chrissie. "You're the piecer now. You'll be responsible for the entire mule, understand? And I don't want to come by here and see any broken threads unless you're already busy fixing them."

Chrissie's heart leaped. "Yes, sir." she cried. "Thank you, sir."

Bertram ignored her, looking at Suzie. "You're no good," he barked. "You're going to go back to working as a scavenger."

Suzie's eyes widened. "But sir, I'm ten years old. I'm too big to fit under the mule."

"Then perhaps you should have done your piecing better," snapped Bertram. He turned and strode away.

Chrissie felt cold all over when she saw the fury in Suzie's eyes. "Suzie, I'm sorry. I told him that you were doing well, and that I was just helping, and—"

"You've ruined everything." Suzie yelled at her. "You're going to get me killed, crawling about under that mule." She gestured furiously. "Why did you have to do that?"

"I just—I just wanted to impress Bertram," Chrissie stammered out.

"Why?" Suzie screamed. "Why would you want to do that?"

"Because—because—" Tears streamed down Chrissie's cheeks. "Because they adopted me as their daughter, and maybe, if I work well enough, they'll take me into their part of the house and send me to school and read me bedtime stories and treat me like their own."

Suzie stared at her, her eyes very hard. "How could you be so stupid?" she hissed. "They never adopted you. They never wanted a *child* of their own. They took you in for the same reason as they took all of us in—to work in the mill. That's all they want. A worker."

"I just want to be their real daughter," Chrissie whispered, tears pouring down her cheeks.

"Well, you aren't," snapped Suzie. "And you never will be."

She grabbed the brush and scoop, gave Chrissie a last baleful look, and crawled beneath the cotton mule.

CHAPTER 8

CHRISSIE DIPPED her rusk into the watery tea. There was no milk or cream in the tea, but she had slurped down half of the cup thirstily. Piecing was hard work; her feet ached, and her fingers had already bled twice today from the fine, cutting cotton threads.

She sucked on the rusk. It was as tasteless as the tea, but even though she had been working since six and it was now about nine, it was her first food for the day. She munched it down hungrily, huddled on a box near the mule, utterly ignored by the other children, who were gathered at the other end of the factory, talking.

The mule was near the back of the factory, and there was a window nearby. Chrissie had opened the door earlier, letting in a little of the fresher, cooler air from outside to dispel some of the dust that hung everywhere in the factory. She could hear snatches of conversation from outside sometimes when the mule was turned off, like now, and she loved listening to people going about their day. People who lived very different lives.

On this day, though, the voice that floated through the window seemed almost familiar. Chrissie closed her eyes, listening to it as she leaned against the wall. It was a man's voice, and it had a rich, country accent, very different from the sharp Cockney she'd been hearing since she came here weeks ago. She couldn't quite make out the words, but it felt good just to listen to that familiarity. It reminded her of Christmas in the countryside, all family gatherings, and friendships.

Footsteps came nearer the wall, and the man's voice became clearer. "… take this shipment to the village by tonight."

Chrissie's eyes popped open. She knew that voice. It belonged to Joe Wilkes, a jack-of-all-trades from her old village. He had mended Papa Roy's roof just a couple of summers ago.

She scrambled to her feet, dragging the box nearer to the window, and stood on it. If she gripped the windowsill, she could just manage to peer over the edge and into the yard behind the factory.

It was Joe all right. The sight of him made her want to cry, even though he was a scruffy character with a gap-toothed grin and red hair that stuck out in all directions. He was helping Bertram to load bolts of cotton onto the back of the wagon.

"Are you sure your master doesn't want to take any more, Mr. Wilkes?" asked Bertram, with his best smile.

Joe shook his head. "Not right now. It's only a little shop, it is, and he can't buy too much at once, he said. But I'm sure I'll be back very soon." Joe patted the bolt of cotton lying on the back of the wagon. "It's nice cotton, and cheaper than anything else we can get in the city."

"That's good to hear." Bertram smiled. "Now, would you like anything before you go?"

"No thank'ee, sir. I'm just goin' to give the old horse a feed of oats, like, and then I'll be off."

"Very well." Bertram shook hands with him. "I hope to see you again very soon."

Bertram walked away, and Joe took a nosebag out from under his seat and slipped it over his dark bay horse's head. The horse began to eat contentedly, and Joe took a pipe out of his pocket and began to fill it.

Chrissie took a deep breath, glancing at the back door of the factory. There were still a few minutes left before her break would be over. With any luck, Bertram wouldn't notice if she spoke to Joe for a few minutes. Joe might know how Jonah was—and Chrissie was desperate to hear anything about him.

She pushed the door open and slipped into the yard, nervously approaching Joe. It seemed so strange to see a piece of her old life standing here in brutal London.

"Mr. Wilkes?" she breathed.

Joe jumped so hard he nearly dropped his pipe. Flakes of tobacco scattered across the floor. "Well, as I live and breathe." he gasped, his eyes wide as they rested on her. "Is it really you, Chrissie Ellis? Roy and Beulah's great-granddaughter?"

"That's me, sir," said Chrissie.

Joe stared at her ragged clothes and her sore hands. "I thought you'd gone to live with a well-to-do solicitor."

"They sent me here, sir," said Chrissie.

Joe sat down sharply on the side of his wagon. "I'll be. Beulah's little girl, working at a cotton mill. She'd be rolling in her grave if she knew." He sighed. "Poor wee thing. I wish I could take you back to the village with me."

Chrissie wished so, too, but she knew no one would take her in. No one had taken her in after Papa Roy died, after all, not even the Costigans.

"I know you can't," she said, and saw relief in his eyes. "But I wanted to hear some news from back home. I... I want to know how Jonah is doing."

"Oh yes," murmured Joe. "He's one of the Costigan boys, isn't he? Poor lad."

"Poor lad?" Chrissie's heart quickened. "Why do you say that?"

"Well, Mr. Costigan died just a few months ago. Cut himself with an ax and bled to death. Terrible, terrible thing," sighed Joe. "The missus is all on her own with the children now, and they've all been put to work."

Chrissie's heart squeezed for Jonah. He'd already been working so hard even before his father had died, and even if Mr. Costigan had been grumpy, Jonah had loved him.

"Would you take a message to Jonah for me?" she asked.

Joe rubbed the back of his neck. "I don't know, missy. I don't have the best memory, you know." He tapped his head.

"You wouldn't have to remember. I'd write it for you," said Chrissie eagerly.

They found a scrap of paper, and Jonah produced a stick of charcoal from the back of his wagon. Chrissie's hand shook as she held the paper against the wall and wrote slowly and carefully, just as Nana had taught her.

Dear Jonah,

I miss you very much and I am sorry to hear about your papa. I work here in a cotton mill in London now. Mr. Wilkes can tell you where. I wish I could see you again and we could make up a story and everything would be all right.

Love,

Chrissie.

She handed the note to Joe. "You'll give it to Jonah, won't you, sir?"

"Of course, I will." Joe nodded vigorously, tucking the note into his pocket.

"Will you be back?" Chrissie asked. "Could you bring a message from him?"

"I'll be here in six months, at the most," Joe promised. "And of course, I'll bring you a message, you poor lamb." He sighed. "You take care of yourself now, little one."

"You too, Mr. Wilkes. I'll see you." *In six months.* It felt like forever, but it was far better than never knowing when she would hear from Jonah again.

The bell rang, and it was time to go to work. "Goodbye, Mr. Wilkes. Thank you." Chrissie gasped, then ran back into the factory.

❧

THE SIX MONTHS dragged by like an eon, but they came to an end at last.

Chrissie choked down her supper of gruel and cheese eagerly, even though every bite was soggy and tasteless. It didn't matter; all that mattered was that, after supper, she would finally have a moment's privacy to read the note that Joe had slipped under the back door of the factory earlier that day. Chrissie's head thumped with pain from the noise of her work, and even her hard and calloused fingers were sore. But she felt as though she was floating above the pain and exhaustion tonight. She was about to hear from Jonah for the first time in more than a year, and she couldn't wait.

Rain fell outside in a steady patter when her meal was done at last, and she could curl up on her pallet. Seeking the sliver of light that came through the crack of the door, Chrissie unfolded the scrap of paper that she'd hidden in the top of her dress, and her eyes slowly began to pick out the words. She had taught Jonah to write herself, and his writing was wobbly and painstaking; it took her some time to string the letters together.

Dere Crisi,

I was so hapy to here from yu. I mis yu very mutch. Nuthing is the same with out yu. Papa is ded and I mis him tu.

One daye I wil see yu agen. I promus yu. I wil find yu wen the littul ones can feed them selfs. I wil not fore get yu. Every thing wil be al rite agen.

Yu are Prinses Crisi. Dunt fore get it.

Love,

Jonah.

Chrissie's eyes stung with happy tears. She pressed the letter close to her chest, then read it again, memorizing every clumsy word. It didn't matter one bit that Jonah couldn't spell. All that mattered was his promise: that he would come to find her someday, and that everything would be all right again.

You are Princess Chrissie. Don't forget it. No one had called her that in a very long time, and the thought sent wonderful warmth spreading through her chest.

❦

CHRISSIE WHISTLED to herself as she hurried down the length of the mule, reaching out quickly to piece a thread. Her fingers were quick and sure, and it was done before the spinning could be interrupted even for a moment. She stood still at the end of the mule, looking down the length of it, whistling a few more bars of "O Holy Night". It was Jonah's favorite Christmas carol, and even though it was late summer now, it had been going through Chrissie's head for weeks ever since Jonah's letter had come.

She glanced around. There was no sign of Bertram; she thought she could hear him yelling angrily from the room next door, where the older girls worked the looms that wove cotton thread into fabric. She reached into the top of her dress, running her fingertips along the seam where she kept the piece of paper.

There was nothing there. Chrissie frowned. That couldn't be possible. She'd read that piece of paper so many times that it had become as soft and thin as a piece of silk—perhaps she just couldn't feel it. She peeped into the top of her dress, searching.

"Are you looking for this?"

Chrissie looked up, the blood draining from her face at the tone of Suzie's voice. Covered in bits of lint and grime, the girl stood a few feet away, her brush and scoop in one hand, and that familiar much-folded, grimy piece of paper in the other.

"Suzie, please." Chrissie's mouth was dry. "Please give it back to me."

"Is it a love letter?" Suzie taunted, waving it. "Is it from your beau?"

"I'm only a young girl. I don't write love letters. It's from a dear friend." Tears flooded Chrissie's eyes. "Please, Suzie, please, give it to me." She held out her hand.

"What, the way you gave me the most dangerous job in the mill?" Suzie shot back.

"I never meant to hurt you," Chrissie sobbed. "Please don't do this. Just give me back my letter."

Suzie's eyes narrowed. "I shan't," she hissed. "I want you to learn your lesson. I want you to know never to cross me again."

"Suzie, please—" Chrissie gasped.

But it was too late. Tucking the brush and scoop under her arm, Suzie gripped the letter in both hands.

"No!" Chrissie cried.

There was no stopping Suzie. With a few brisk movements, she tore the worn paper to shreds and cast it into the garbage.

"No. No." Chrissie sobbed, running over to the garbage bag and grasping for the scraps, but each was the size of her fingernail. She caught only a glimpse of a few faded letters in his wobbly writing.

"What's going on back there?" Bertram thundered.

Chrissie stared up at Suzie. In the moment before they both had to hurry back to work, she saw just one thing in the other girl's eyes: baleful triumph.

They hurried back to the mule, Chrissie's eyes blurred with tears even as she hastened to piece a thread. As she always did when she was upset, she reached for Jonah's letter. But it was gone.

It was like losing him all over again.

SWEAT POURED down Jonah's brow, stinging his eyes. He paused to wipe it away, leaning on a pitchfork in the blistering sun, his body trembling with exhaustion. Farmer Green had told him that he would pay him a few more pennies each week—but only if he would do the work of two farm hands. What choice did he have? His mother and siblings were starving.

Turning back to the stack of hay on the wagon, Jonah thrust the pitchfork into it and lifted a huge pile from the wagon. It was so heavy that his hands trembled, reddening on the handle of the fork, but Jonah gritted his teeth and forced his aching muscles to lift the pile through the loft window and thrust it inside. Not allowing himself to take another breather, Jonah shoved the fork into the hay again, threw another forkful into the loft.

It was so hot. He was so thirsty, but there was no time to stop for a break, or Farmer Green would be angry. And if Farmer Green was angry, he might lose his work. And if he lost his work, what would his littlest siblings eat? What would his mother do? The look in her eyes had been frightening him lately.

As he always did when the work became too much, Jonah allowed his heart to take wing and fly away, far from this sweltering sun and this wagon, all the way to London and a cotton mill where Chrissie worked. He allowed himself to remember the way her cheeks dimpled when she laughed and the gentleness in her voice when she called him "Prince

Jonah." A smile tugged at his lips then, despite his suffering, and he longed to see her again. Soon. As soon as all the little ones could work, Jonah would go and find her, and everything would be better.

"Are you Jonah Costigan?"

Jonah stopped, leaning on his pitchfork, and looked toward the voice that had spoken from the farm gate. For an awful second, he thought he was looking at Chrissie; a terribly, terribly wasted version of Chrissie, with her dress hanging from her bony frame in tattered rags, her eyes bloodshot and filmy, her mouth turned down deeply at the corners. Then he realized that it wasn't a girl standing at the gate, but a woman in her twenties.

His thundering heart slowed only slightly. She had Chrissie's eyes.

"I am," Jonah said. "Who are you?"

"You won't know me. I'm looking for Christmas Ellis," said the woman.

Jonah narrowed his eyes. "If I don't know you, then tell me who you are."

The woman's mouth twisted. "What's it to you?"

Jonah shoved the fork back into the hay. "If you won't tell me, then I won't tell you a thing."

"Very well. My name is Dovie Brentcliff, if you must know. Christmas is my daughter. Is that such a crime, for a mother to be looking for her daughter?" Dovie shot back.

Jonah stopped, staring at her. He'd heard about Dovie, of course. Everyone in the village muttered about her—Jonah had spent much of his time trying to protect Chrissie from the things people said about her. Judging by the hardness in her eyes, at least some of those things had come true.

"What do you want with Chrissie?" he asked.

The woman's eyes narrowed. "So you *do* know her."

Jonah waited. Dovie folded her arms. "I want my daughter back, that's what. She must be nine now, almost ten? And a pretty little thing, isn't she?"

The way she said it made something twist deep in Jonah's gut. He didn't know exactly what Dovie wanted with Chrissie, but he was certain, from the look in her eyes, that it was nothing good.

"The prettiest thing you ever saw," he told her.

"Where is she?" Dovie demanded.

Jonah took a deep breath. "I don't know."

Dovie scoffed. "So how do you know her, then?"

"She left here almost a year ago now. Roy and Beulah Ellis died, and she had to go and live with someone else. I don't know who, and I don't know where she is. I haven't seen her since." Jonah's stomach clenched at the lie, but he would do it to keep Chrissie safe.

Dovie stared at him for a few more moments out of those bloodshot eyes. Then she shrugged, turned around, and walked away.

Jonah squeezed his eyes tightly shut. *Dear God, please, help Chrissie. Keep her safe.* He felt a sudden urge to rush to the address Joe Wilkes had told him, to tell Chrissie about Dovie, to warn her to stay away from her mother no matter how much she wanted to go with her.

But if he left now, his family would starve. He could only hope that his lie would be enough to protect her.

PART IV

CHAPTER 9

Three Years Later

CHRISSIE WALKED down the line of cotton bales, counting softly under her breath. She paused at the end of the row, glancing down at the notebook in her hands. Frowning, she scribbled a number. There were twenty-five cotton bales in this row, and there was supposed to be twenty-six. Charlie must have made a mistake on the stacking again.

She sighed, knowing that she had to go into the weaving room and confront him. Tipping up her chin, she clutched the notebook tightly and went through to Bertram's new office. It was part of the extension he'd built onto the cotton mill, and still smelled of new wood when Chrissie knocked at the door.

"What is it?" Bertram demanded.

Chrissie pushed the door slightly open, holding up the notebook. "I'm sorry, sir. There are only twenty-five bales in Warehouse B. There should be twenty-six."

Bertram's sudden smile made her heart leap. "You're such a clever little thing, Christmas. It's hard to believe that you're only twelve."

Almost twelve, Chrissie thought. Christmas was still three days away.

"Well, go and speak with Charlie about it, then. Find out where that other bale is." Bertram turned his attention back to his work.

"Yes, sir." Chrissie sighed, heading back to the weaving room. She'd hoped Bertram would be angry enough to confront Charlie himself, but clearly—as usual—he was quite happy to leave Chrissie to do most of the work in her role as manager of the weaving room.

She stepped into the dark, hot room, sneezing as she breathed a cloud of dust. The enormous looms clacked loudly as they worked, rows of them in the long, low room, turning threads into fabric with their long, spidery arms that moved with an alien, mechanical efficiency in the gloom. Charlie was at the back of the room, tying up the piles of fabric into bales. He was several years older than Chrissie—almost a man himself—

and there was a dangerous glitter in his eyes as she approached him.

She drew herself up to her full height. "Charlie, I need to speak with you."

Charlie sighed, rolling his eyes, and didn't slow down as he continued baling the fabric. "What do you want?"

"I would like to know why we are missing a bale in Warehouse B." Chrissie squared her shoulders.

"I don't know," said Charlie. "Look in those clever little notebooks of yours." He sneered with the disdain of the utterly illiterate.

Chrissie gritted her teeth. "I have looked. That's why I know there should be twenty-six bales in there. Did you leave one of the bales from yesterday in the weaving room?" She glanced into the corner where Charlie sometimes liked to shove bales under a table when he was too lazy to carry them over to Warehouse B.

"What's it to you if I did?" Charlie shooed her away. "Go play somewhere else, little girl."

Chrissie's heart stung at his words. Couldn't they all just get along? She tipped up her chin, not backing down. "You know my records are never wrong, Charlie. And you know that you'll be in trouble with the boss if you don't get that bale into that warehouse by the time I count the stock again tonight."

Charlie's eyes glinted all the more, because Chrissie knew she was right.

"You think you're so special," he hissed. "You think you're smarter than all of us just because the boss treats you different. Well, you're just another wretch in a cotton mill just like the rest of us. And one day Mr. Jones will realize that you're worthless."

Chrissie's heart stung painfully at his words. "Just make sure that bale gets to the warehouse," she said, and hurried away to check on the looms.

Worthless. The word echoed through her mind. Maybe Charlie was right—after all, her mother, her grandmother, and Theodore all thought she wasn't good enough to keep. Blinking away tears, Chrissie paused in a corner of the warehouse and pulled out the latest letter from Jonah. His writing skills had improved over the past three years, and she smiled as she read.

Dear Princess Chrissie,

I am so happy to heer about yer new job as the manager of the weeving room. You deserv it. I'm glad they r giving you sum money now. Make shure you have everything you need.

My savings are goin' a little better now. I hope someday to have enuf to buy a ticket to London and come to see you. I miss you so much and nevr stop thinking about you.

Peggy will go to werk in the next year. It won't be long befor I can come to find you, I pray.

May God be with you.

Love,

Jonah

The letter was old now, the words faded, the corners fuzzy with constant folding and unfolding. Chrissie smoothed it between her fingers, smiling. Any day now, Joe would be back for his biannual shipment, and she would have a new letter from Jonah. She could easily scribble her response in her notebook and give it to Joe. She couldn't wait to hear from him.

In fact, at that moment, she heard the rumble of a wagon approaching the courtyard, and her heart turned over. It had to be Joe.

She rushed out into the courtyard, her heart pounding, and sighed when the horse coming into the courtyard was grey instead of bay. Its driver, too, was far younger than Joe, and had a natty little moustache, his hat cocked jauntily at an angle on his head.

"Good morning," she said boldly. "Are you here for a shipment?"

The young man laughed at her. "And who are you, you precious little thing?"

Chrissie gave him a brittle smile. "I'm the manager of the weaving room and warehouses here. Are you here for a shipment?"

The young man's smile slipped. "You must be joking."

"I'm not." Chrissie kept her smile in place.

The young man shrugged, stopping the wagon. "All right. Yes, I'm here for a shipment. For Mr. Bobby Hanks."

Chrissie's heart stopped. Bobby Hanks was the shopkeeper in her old village. "Where's Joe?" she gasped. "Joe Wilkes?"

"Poor old Joe," said the young man. "He's dead."

"Dead?" Chrissie cried.

"As a doornail. Smallpox." The young man shrugged. "I'm his replacement. So, where should I stop the wagon?"

Chrissie's heart thundered. Joe, dead. How would she get letters to Jonah now? Bobby Hanks had never known about their arrangement; Joe used to deliver her messages to Jonah himself.

"Do you know Jonah Costigan?" she asked.

"I'm not even from the village." The young man laughed. "I only stop by there on my way to other places."

Chrissie's heart sank to her boots as the young man turned away and began to attend to the horse. She stumbled back into the factory. What would she do now?

Smallpox. She'd heard of it before, of course. Some of the girls who worked here had lost both of their parents and all of their siblings to it; one of them, Diana, still bore smallpox scars all over her own face. It was very catching, and it was very deadly, and it was in the village if it had killed Joe.

The next thought that crossed Chrissie's mind almost made her drop her notebook. She stood in the warehouse, frozen in place, her heart thundering wildly.

What if Jonah had caught it?

Tears swarmed her eyes. Jonah could be sick at this very moment... or worse. Far worse. She hadn't heard from him in six months. So much could have happened in between.

She stumbled deeper into the warehouse on shaky legs and sank down on one of the bales of fabric, her shaking fingers going numb.

I'll find you. I promise. Jonah's promise was the one light in her life ever since she'd been taken from Theodore's house. Ever since she had come to this dark place. And if Jonah was dead, then the light was gone. Then she had no one left in the whole world who loved her.

She had to know. She had to find out. The terror gripped her at the same time as the wild idea leaped into her mind, watching as the young man flipped a heavy canvas cover off the back of the wagon, shaking snow aside.

Revealing plenty of little dark places inside. Places where a small, thin girl like Chrissie could easily hide.

CHAPTER 10

CHRISSIE WAITED UNTIL SIX O' clock the next morning.

The young man and his horse had gone off to an inn for the night, and they would be back at dawn to start their long journey. At six, the workers all streamed into the factory, the furnaces were fired up to power the steam-driven mule, and noise and activity filled that dank and dusty place. And Chrissie went up and down in the weaving room, checking that all the looms were functional and that all the workers were doing their part. She could feel their angry eyes following her around the room as she watched them.

It didn't matter that they hated her, not so long as Jonah loved her. But Jonah could be dead now, or... or perhaps he had found another girl to love. One that was close by; one that he could hold in his arms. He was fifteen by now, after all. Maybe he wouldn't wait forever.

The doubts and fears crashed in Chrissie's heart, making it grow bigger and bigger until it felt as though it would explode with the sheer tumult of emotions inside her. She took deep breaths, glancing out of the window at the wagon, already loaded, the canvas stretched tight over the bales.

There was no other way.

As soon as the weaving room was well underway, and every pair of eyes was turned to their work, Chrissie knew she couldn't wait a moment longer. She closed her notebook neatly and set it down on a fabric bale where it would be easily found. Someone else would have to write in it for the next two days. Then she turned and hurried out into the yard, a collection of black shapes in the darkness, only a few squares of light cast by the factory windows guiding her way to the hulking shape of the wagon, illuminated by one of the windows. She hesitated in the shadows, glancing up at the window. Was Bertram looking out at her right now? What would he do if he found her?

She didn't want to find out. Seeing no face at the window, Chrissie bolted forward. She seized the corner of the canvas and flipped it back, spotting a hiding place near the back of the wagon, where the bales had not been pushed all the way into the corner. Sucking in a breath, Chrissie squeezed her way between the bales and the canvas. They scraped roughly against her face and knees and elbows, the canvas catching her hair and pulling it, but she kicked and squirmed and kept going until she had made it to the hiding place in the very back.

It was just about big enough. She pushed at some of the bales, buying herself an extra few inches so that she could squeeze herself into the little hole. It smelled dusty and dry in here, and Chrissie could only pray that no one would notice the rumpled canvas. Or that she was gone.

She squeezed her eyes tightly shut, gripped by terror, tears stinging. Was this insanity? What would Bertram and Chloe do when she returned? She took a deep breath, shaking all over. Perhaps it was insanity, but either way, she had to see Jonah. She had to find him and make sure he was all right.

It was what Princess Chrissie would do.

The memory of his voice saying those words, *Princess Chrissie*, was the only thing that stopped her from crawling right out from her hiding spot and fleeing back into the predictable routine of her day at the cotton mill when she heard the thud of hoofbeats and felt the jolt of the wagon as it was harnessed. It was the only thing that stopped her from screaming when she felt a sharp tug at the canvas, almost crushing her, as it was tightened over the bales.

And it was the only thing that kept her there, cowering and determined, as the wagon began to move. There was a tiny tear in the canvas nearby, and she crawled over to it, peering through the rip at the squat shape of the cotton mill as it was left further and further behind until the wagon turned a corner and, for the first time in three years, Chrissie was out of sight of the mill.

CHRISSIE WAS INSANE.

She knew it; she had to be. She had been beaten before, but only once, when Suzie had convinced Bertram that Chrissie had fallen asleep on the job, back when she was still a piecer. As Chrissie lay in the jolting, bumping wagon, her joints aching from being crammed in amongst the bales, she remembered every thump of Bertram's belt slapping into the bare skin of her back. She remembered the black bruises that had covered her back, and the bitter tears she'd wept on her pallet that night, too sore to sleep, too exhausted to stay awake.

The same thing would happen to her when she got back, she knew it, and that was if she survived the journey. Chrissie had no idea how much time had passed since she had crawled into the wagon. Whenever she looked out of the tear in the canvas now, she saw only blackness. The wagon moved painfully slowly compared to the stagecoach that had brought her to London all those years ago.

Another bump shook the entire wagon, rattling Chrissie's aching bones. She bit back a cry of pain, although her throat was so dry, she doubted a single sound could escape. It felt as though the dust from the bales had all gone into her throat and settled there, and though she swallowed and swallowed, it only made her thirst grow steadily worse. Hunger pangs assailed her entire body, running up and down to her chest and legs from her stomach.

She pillowed her head against the corner of a bale and tried again to sleep. The first few hours of the wagon ride had been blissful; Chrissie couldn't remember when last she had been allowed to sleep for as long as she wanted. But now her body hurt too much, and she simply lay there, exhausted and scared, wondering what would happen to her. Wondering if the wagon would even stop in her village at all, or if it would come to a halt on some alien planet, somewhere completely new and terrifying, somewhere that—

The wagon jolted to a halt, slamming Chrissie against its wooden back. She let out a gasp, shaking herself. Somehow, she'd fallen asleep again after all. Now, she was surrounded by voices.

"What do you mean by this, arriving at ten o' clock at night?"

Chrissie's heart leaped into her mouth. She knew that voice; she had spoken with it a thousand times, buying fabric to mend Papa Roy's shirts or to make Nana Beulah a new dress. It was Bobby Hanks.

She was home.

"The roads were slippery," the young man protested. "It's a bad time of year for shipments. Come on, Bobby. It's right before Christmas."

"I've a mind to dock your wages for this," Bobby grumbled. "And that's Mr. Hanks to you. Now let's unload this—or do you want to stand here in the cold until midnight?"

"Aw, Mr. Hanks, can't a man have a cup of hot tea after a long cold day on the road first?" the young man wheedled.

Chrissie squeezed her eyes tightly shut. *Please, please say yes,* she begged Bobby silently. If he agreed, then Chrissie would have a moment to slip away without being seen.

Bobby sighed. "All right, then. Come on."

Their footsteps crunched away in the snow, and Chrissie waited until she could no longer hear them before she stirred her stiff and tired limbs to action. The act of crawling through those bales was excruciating. Her poor, sore joints screamed in protest, making her limbs tremble with agony as she squeezed herself through the narrowest gaps across the wagon. When she reached the end, she found the canvas tied down tightly, and knew a moment of utter panic until she found she could slip her thin wrist underneath it and pull at the knots that held it down.

At last, wonderfully, the canvas gave way. Fresh, icy air rushed into Chrissie's lungs, and she tumbled out onto the snow, landing on her hands and knees. It was so blessedly wonderful to be able to see all around her and to breathe fresh air that she nearly cried. She spent several seconds like that, sucking in great gasps of air, coughing, and staring down at the bright white snow in the light from Bobby's flat over his shop.

Voices from the flat urged her to her feet. She staggered out of the little yard behind Bobby's shop and out into the street of her own home village, the village she hadn't seen since Mrs. Costigan took her to live with Theodore, and for a few moments she could do nothing other than to stand and stare. She had never seen anything so magical in all her life. The little houses that lined the handful of streets were all generously dusted with snow; not the dirty, yellowish stuff you got in London, but real, white, sparkling snow that shimmered in the light of the full moon overhead. Golden firelight leaped in the windows from the candles in every windowsill, and wherever Chrissie looked, wreaths hung on the doors, all bright with holly and ribbons.

As she stumbled down the street, gazing at the glory around her, Chrissie was unsurprised to see the Christmas tree in the market square ahead of her. A fine, tall, straight conifer, it was all hung as usual with ribbons and paper chains, even though those had grown a little soggy from the snow. And there was a star made of holly berries attached to some twisted wire at the very top, seeming to glow softly in the moonlight.

Gazing up at the tree, Chrissie felt that it was Christmas again for the very first time since she had left the village she loved.

She looked up the street, toward her old home. She did not allow her eyes to rest on the cottage where she and Papa and Nana had been so happy together. Instead, she set her eyes on the Costigan house, and strode toward it with quick, sure steps, her heart thundering behind her ribs.

The moment that passed between her knocking upon the door and it finally opening seemed to be the longest interval of Chrissie's entire life. And when the door swung open at last, it was as though her entire world came to a complete halt. Jonah stood in the doorway, looking down at her with his soft eyes, and he was so much bigger and taller than she remembered and there was a prickling of hair growing on his upper lip, but he was still Jonah, her Jonah, alive and well and in the flesh. She felt her heart turn a wild cartwheel inside her chest, and the glad cry tore from her before she could stop it.

"Oh, Jonah, Jonah," she cried, and flung her arms around him.

Jonah returned her embrace, trembling in her arms, and he smelled the way he always had; of roast chestnuts and pine needles. "Chrissie?" He gasped. "Is it you?"

She stepped back, smiling up at him. "Yes. Yes, it's me."

He stared at her, his eyes alight with joy for a few moments before fear stole across them. Darting out of the house, he pulled the door shut behind him, but did not let go of her hand. "I couldn't send you a letter. Joe died, and the young man who takes Mr. Hanks' shipments laughed at me when I asked him."

The young man had lied when he had said that he didn't know a Jonah Costigan. The thought made Chrissie's heart sting, but nothing could hurt her too much right now, not when she was looking into his eyes. "I didn't know if you were all right. He said Joe had died of smallpox, and I was so afraid that something had happened to you. But nothing has," she cried. "And you're here, and I'm here."

Jonah laughed with joy, a single tear escaping down his cheek. "I missed you so much, Princess Chrissie. I'm so glad you're here." He hugged her again and held her tightly for even longer this time. Chrissie had not been hugged since Papa Roy died. It felt more wonderful than she could ever have described.

When Jonah let her go, however, there was regret on his face. "I wish I could bring you inside, but Mama... she's sick. I don't know what's wrong with her. I don't know if it's catching, and she couldn't accept you inside... not after Papa died."

"I'm sorry." Chrissie tried not to let her fear show in her eyes. If she couldn't come in, where would she stay the night?

"Don't worry." Jonah took her hand firmly, as though he had read her thoughts. "We can hide in Farmer Green's loft. He won't know a thing."

FARMER GREEN'S loft smelled sweetly of hay and apples. Chrissie sat curled up against a pile of hay, eating an apple in hungry bites, her hunger quickly overwhelming her guilt at taking one. She hadn't eaten since the night before.

The ladder creaked, and Jonah plodded up into the loft, carrying a horse blanket. "Here—it smells like a horse, but it's warm." He sat down beside it, shaking it open in a cloud of horse fur. Chrissie sneezed.

Jonah laughed, wrapping one end around her shoulders. "Warm enough?"

Chrissie looked up into his soft eyes. "Yes," she whispered.

Jonah grinned. He sat down beside her, wrapping the blanket around them both. "I can't believe you came all that way. You're so brave, Chrissie."

Chrissie leaned her head on his shoulder. "I had to see you. I had to know that you were all right."

"Oh, Chrissie, I'm so glad to see you. You have no idea how I've missed you." Jonah tucked the blanket down around her shoulders a little more tightly. "It's been so, so long." He sighed. "I can't believe that solicitor sent you off to London. I saw his children in the village one day, when I went there with Farmer Green to a horse sale, and they're so plump and well-dressed and—and you should have been with them."

Chrissie sighed. "I don't know what I did wrong for him to send me away."

"You did nothing wrong," said Jonah. "I promise you that."

The way he said it made her want to believe it was true. She smiled, closing her eyes. It was so good to be beside him.

"Maybe I don't have to go back," she whispered.

Jonah hesitated. "I'm so sorry. My mama..."

"I know I can't stay with you, even though I wish I could." Chrissie sighed. "But I could look for work in the village. Surely someone needs a girl to sweep their floors or wash their clothes. I can read and write, maybe I can even work in a shop, or..."

"I'm sorry, Chrissie." Jonah sighed. "The village isn't the same since the smallpox outbreak. So many of us are out of work. Two of my siblings, even."

Chrissie knew Jonah had been struggling even before then. "I'm sorry."

"It's all right. I just wish you could stay." He sighed. "But you have a good job in London... and someday things will be better. Someday I'll come to find you, and we'll have a cottage of our own."

"A cottage of our very own." Chrissie smiled. "With a little field in the back, and a big tree to climb, and a stream at the bottom for ice skating."

Jonah laughed. "Yes, exactly like that."

It sounded like the fairy tales they used to tell one another when they were little children, but Chrissie enjoyed dreaming of it in any case. They sat together in silence for a while, Chrissie nibbling apples and beginning to fall asleep on Jonah's shoulder.

She had just begun to drift into a doze when he spoke. "Have you... have you seen Dovie?"

"Dovie?" Chrissie sat upright. "My mother?"

Jonah met her eyes, and there was something very serious in them that made Chrissie's heart beat faster. "No... no. I haven't seen her... in my life, I suppose, apart from being born." She frowned. "Why?"

"Oh, no reason." Jonah held out the blanket. "Come now. Go back to sleep. I'm sorry I woke you."

Chrissie didn't move. "Have you seen my mother?"

He looked away. "I just want to keep you safe."

She stared at him. "Jonah... what is it? Please. Tell me." Her eyes stung with tears. "Please, Jonah."

He looked down at the ground, sighing. "I don't want to keep secrets from you..."

"Then don't. Please."

"All right." Jonah took a long breath. "I saw your mother."

"When?" Chrissie gasped.

"Once, almost three years ago, right after I'd gotten your first letter." Jonah finally met her eyes. "And the other time was about four months ago."

"You saw her, and you didn't tell me?" Chrissie cried. "Why?"

"Because I don't think you're safe with her," said Jonah. "Please, Chrissie, don't be upset. I'm telling you now."

She bit her lip. "I'm not upset with you. I'm just—so surprised. Oh, Jonah, what was she like? What did she want? Did she talk to you?"

"She did," Jonah said. "She was looking for you."

"Looking for me." Chrissie cried, excitement leaping in her heart. "Did you tell her where to find me?"

Jonah shook his head. "She... she wasn't nice, Chrissie. She was thin and hard, and she seemed worn down and desperate." His eyes were steady on hers. "Desperate people do cruel things. I think she was working..." He cleared his throat. "You know. On the streets."

Chrissie sat in silence with that thought. Her mother, working on the streets? She'd seen women on the street corner near the factory sometimes, seen them go into the building with men who would give them money. She could imagine, more or less, what they really did. But the revelation was nothing in comparison to the idea that her mother existed and was someone real and concrete.

"I can't believe my mother is looking for me," she gasped. "Oh, Jonah, maybe she loves me and misses me after all."

"Chrissie, I don't think..." Jonah began.

"Maybe she wants to be a mother to me," Chrissie cried. "Maybe she wants us to be a family. Maybe whatever was wrong with me that made her go away in the first place is better now, and she wants me back." Tears filled her eyes at the thought.

"I don't think you should go looking for her," said Jonah. "I don't think it's safe. I think she wants to use you somehow."

Chrissie knew, though his words seemed harsh, that Jonah only wanted to protect her. It made it difficult to be angry with him, but still, she couldn't release the spark of hope in her heart. It burned brightly, keeping her warm that Christmas Eve as she slept upon the hay, as a babe in a manger had once slept many, many years ago.

CHAPTER 11

CHRISSIE'S HAND trembled in Jonah's as they walked across the market square.

"It'll be all right," he murmured over and over. "Everything will be all right."

She couldn't stop thinking about how Theodore had said the same thing to her, right before stuffing her into the stagecoach that had taken her to London. It was snowing in big, fat, white flakes that drifted down slowly, as though to show the world how very beautiful they were, each one unique and shining. One landed on Chrissie's cheek, and Jonah brushed it off with a mittened hand before it could melt.

"Don't be scared, Chrissie," he said softly. "It's going to be all right."

On the other side of the square, a jolly man was harnessing his cart to a piebald horse. The man's clothes were all tattered, and when his wife stepped out of the house beside him, her red coat was faded and much-patched; but they both smiled despite the age that grizzled the wife's hair and the man's beard.

"You must be Chrissie," said the man, giving Chrissie a big smile. "Welcome on board."

"Thank you very much for letting me ride with you," said Christmas.

The wife chuckled. "Isn't she precious. Of course, pet. If we have to drive all the way into London to see our family on Christmas Day, you may as well come along."

"And it was good of you to give us tuppence for our trouble, young man." The man gave Jonah a little bow.

Jonah had arranged it all that morning; Chrissie didn't know where he'd found tuppence, but she was grateful he had.

"Are you ready to go?" asked the man.

Chrissie couldn't bring herself to let go of Jonah's hand. She tightened her grip on it, turning to him. "Oh, Jonah, will I ever see you again?"

"Of course, you will." Jonah took both of her hands and squeezed them. "I promised to find you, don't you remember?

And I'll post my letters this time, so they will find you. I know they will."

Chrissie managed a smile, but she didn't want to let go of his hands.

"Wait a minute." Jonah reached into his pocket and pulled out a folded piece of paper. "Here—it's the letter I never got to send you." He pressed it into her hand. "You can read it when you get to London, and it will feel a little more like I'm with you."

"Thank you," Chrissie whispered. She felt slightly better. "And I'll write back at once. And I'll send you money, for the stamps."

"Thank you, Chrissie." Jonah put his arms around her and kissed her forehead, and it made her feel wonderfully warm all up and down her body. "Goodbye."

She couldn't help it. The sound of the word made tears pour down her cheeks. They came so thickly and so quickly that she could not stop them, that she could not say it back, that she clambered in silence into the jolly man's wagon and stared back at Jonah as he waved and waved under the glowing Christmas tree.

CHRISSIE HAD NEVER SEEN London so dark. In fact, she had never seen this part of London at all.

"You can't miss it," said the jolly man, pointing at the spot on the map he'd marked with an X. "See? You just have to keep going down this street, then you'll get to the factories. And as soon as you turn onto Star Road, you'll recognize the street. You'll be home in a jiff."

Chrissie stared up at him mutely, wishing that he wouldn't go. They had stopped by a crossroads; the jolly man and his wife were heading deeper into the city, and their ways would part here. Chrissie would have to make the rest of this journey on her own.

"Off you go then, dear." The jolly man gave her a pat on the head. "You'll be fine."

He turned and clambered back onto his cart and slapped the reins on the tired piebald horse's back, and the animal plodded resolutely forward, quickly swallowed up by the darkness.

Chrissie stood in a pool of yellow streetlight, taking deep, frightened breaths as she gazed at the street ahead of her. The man had said she just needed to keep going down this street until she saw Star Road. But how long would that take? All night?

She squeezed her eyes tightly shut, wishing that she had never left Jonah's warm barn. Wishing that she had stayed in the village, where she knew where everything was and where everyone lived, where a friend was never far away. But those friends wouldn't feed her. Only the city would. So Chrissie sucked in a long breath, pulled her coat tightly around herself against the fierce cold, and stumbled forward on her numb legs to face whatever fate awaited her.

The more she walked, the more the city began to change around her. The street lamps grew further and further apart, so that there were times when Chrissie was walking in almost perfect darkness. Shops and businesses around her gave way to towering factories and warehouses, all grim and cold, with narrow alleyways between them that gave out a noisome stench as she walked past. On this Christmas night, not a single light was on in any of the windows, and not a soul stirred. Not even a star shone ahead. Chrissie was absolutely alone.

So she believed, at least, until she heard a scraping from an alleyway as she passed. "That's a nice little coat you've got there, missy," hissed a voice.

Chrissie jumped and looked down into a pair of yellowed eyes topped by a wild mop of grey hair. These belonged to an old woman who sat huddled against the wall, little more than a bundle of bones and rags.

"Th-thank you." Chrissie stepped aside.

"Won't you give it to a cold old woman on a Christmas night?" the woman hissed, snatching at the hem.

"I—I'm—I don't know," Chrissie whimpered.

The woman smiled, but she had no teeth except for one, a blackened thing that trembled in her mouth. She half-crawled toward Chrissie, snatching at her coat. "Give it to me."

"Leave me alone!" Chrissie gasped, frightened.

The woman's iron claws closed on the hem of her coat. She screamed, stumbling back, ripping it from the old vagrant's hands. The woman snatched at her again, scratching her leg this time, hard enough that Chrissie cried out in pain. She turned and bolted down the street as fast as her legs could carry her, her heart pounding wildly, feeling more afraid and alone than ever before in her life.

At last, blessedly, she saw the words on a signpost beneath a streetlamp dead ahead: STAR ROAD. With a cry of relief, Chrissie flung herself down the street, and instantly recognized the silhouette of the cotton mill and the towering shape of the tenement building. It was a hateful place, but at least she knew it, and that made it feel almost like home. She was sure the woman was no longer chasing her, but she still ran all the way up the street and to the door of the tenement, letting herself in with a crash.

Without slowing down, Chrissie bounded up the stairs to the Joneses' tenement three flights up. Her heart was hammering in her throat, pounding with wild relief, when she reached the front door. She knocked on it quickly, hoping that it was still early enough for the Joneses to be awake.

It was. The door swung open, and Chrissie was looking into Chloe's cold eyes.

"Mrs. Jones..." Chrissie gasped. Tears of relief ran down her cheeks. "Mrs. Jones, I'm here. I'm sorry I was gone, but now I'm back, I'm back."

Chloe stared at her for a few long moments. Then she drew back her hand and struck Chrissie. The woman's bony knuckles slapped across Chrissie's cheekbones with slicing pain, and she staggered back, crying out, clutching at her throbbing cheeks.

"Chloe? Who is it?" Bertram rumbled.

Chrissie's limbs were gripped with the sudden urge to run. Instead, she froze in place. Bertram would let her in. He knew how hard she worked, how good she was. He knew that the mill needed her.

"It's *her*," Chloe spat.

Bertram stepped into the doorway, and a single glance into his protruding eyes made Chrissie's heart freeze within her choice.

"I can explain," she blurted out. "Please. I had to go. But I'm back, now, and I'll never run off again. Never. Please just let me in... let me go to sleep in my room and work in the morning. Please."

Bertram reached out and seized Chrissie by the wrist in an iron grip. "You think that's how it works, do you? You think you can just come back here and go on as if nothing ever happened?"

Chrissie turned her face away, trembling, feeling the globules of his spit splash against her face.

Bertram pushed her away, sending her stumbling against the opposite wall. Then he took off his belt and looped it in his hands.

"Please," Chrissie whimpered, but she knew it was coming, that she couldn't stop it. "Please."

Bertram landed the first blow across her chest. She screamed in pain, wrapped her arms around herself and turned around, surrendering her back to the beating. The leather slapped against her skin once, hard enough that she had to suck desperately for air. Then again. Then again. When Bertram had landed five blows on her, Chrissie was down on her knees, sobbing and desperate.

She waited on her hands and knees, cowering and afraid, for him to tell her to get back inside the tenement and go to bed hungry. Instead, when Bertram stepped back, breathing heavily, and put his belt back on, his words sent a terrible chill through her. "Now get out of my sight."

She raised her head, her dirty hair hanging around her face. "Sir?"

"You heard him," Chloe hissed. "Get out of this building."

"But—but where will I sleep?" Chrissie gasped.

"I don't care. You don't work for me anymore." Bertram turned and stomped back into the tenement.

Chrissie's breaths came in broken gasps. "What—what does he mean?" she cried.

"He means you're dismissed," Chloe spat. "We don't want you anymore. You're just not good enough."

Chrissie felt as though her knees were rooted to the floor. Her world swirled with terror. "What?" she whispered.

"You heard him." Chloe waved a hand at her. "Now get out of here. Go away or I'll have him hit you again. Go."

The viciousness in Chloe's voice drove Chrissie to her feet despite her throbbing body. She knew she couldn't take another blow, and so even though she barely knew what was happening, she stumbled down the hallway, down the three flights of stairs, and out into the freezing winter night.

Standing on the street, Chrissie stopped to catch her breath, hugging her aching body, shaking all over. Chloe and Bertram had thrown her away. She had nowhere to go, nowhere to get food, nowhere to sleep out of the snow.

She was truly alone now.

No... not quite. Reaching into her pocket, Chrissie pulled out the letter that Jonah had given her. Tears blurred her eyes so that she could only read the first two words.

Princess Chrissie.

A deep breath lifted her chest, and Chrissie turned her face into the wind. It was time to be Princess Chrissie: to be brave, and to look for another way out.

Maybe she wants to be a mother to me.

It was the only scrap of hope that Chrissie had left. So she clung to it, bent her resolve around it, and strode out into the city to find her mother.

PART V

CHAPTER 12

Two Years Later

CHRISSIE'S entire life was contained in the canvas bag, and there was a hole in the bottom of it. She made sure to put her blanket—the best thing she owned—at the very bottom of the bag, so that nothing else would fall out. There was little else, in any case. A pair of holey socks she had bought from another beggar one lucky day; half of a bun, grown stale and hard now; tuppence; and her letters from Jonah, all ancient and well-thumbed and fuzzy at the edges now, but bound together with a bit of string and wrapped in a rag to keep them as safe as she could.

Chrissie brushed her fingertips across the little bundle of letters, allowing the tiniest smile to touch her lips before she slung the bag over her shoulder and strode out into the day.

She had lost count of all the places in London she had seen. Perhaps this was not her first time in this marketplace, a muddy, squalid place, with puddles of slush lining the foot-paths that led from one ramshackle stall to the other. The stalls themselves were piteous things, cobbled together from sticks and rags and little bits of scrap wood. A hollow-eyed woman sold watery fish soup on one corner; a rag-and-bone man tried to sell his scraps on the other. In between was an assortment of the utterly impoverished, trying desperately to eke out a living.

"Oranges. Lovely oranges," called a little girl on the sidewalk as Chrissie approached her.

She held a shrivelled orange in each hand and a look of total desperation in her eyes, and Chrissie almost spent tuppence on one of those ugly oranges. It must be close to Christmas, then, she thought, if there were oranges for sale in a street like this one. She turned away from the girl and walked away quickly, a hand pressed deep into the pocket of her tattered coat, which was now too small to close around her front. She would be fourteen this Christmas. She wondered if she would live to see it.

Pushing the thought aside, Chrissie limped down the street on frostbitten feet, her face set as always to the south, carrying her further and further from the village. In the first year she had lived on the street, Chrissie had tried to stay as far north as she could while she searched for Dovie. Surely Dovie must come from the north, if she'd gone up to the village to see Jonah. And Chrissie had clung to the hope that maybe, someday, she would scrounge together enough money from begging to be able to get a ride back to the village. But the years had come and gone, and the best she could do was scrape together the pennies to write to Jonah from time to time, even though there was nowhere for him to write back to.

She shook off the thought, grasping at a scrap of hope as she stumbled southward. It was the same scrap she had clung to for the two long, long years that had passed: the hope that Dovie might be around the very next corner.

Her tired feet took her to the docks, which were slick with ice, the ships floating on slushy waters, their rigging stiff and frozen, their sails dusted with frost. A few men leered at her as she plodded along, and she held her bag close, pulled her jacket a little more tightly around her body. The old man who sold tiny fish at the marketplace had said that he'd seen a knot of women on the docks just a few streets away, that one of them had looked just like Chrissie. She had no idea what Dovie looked like, but Nana Beulah used to tell her sometimes that she had Dovie's eyes. It was the best guess she had, the most solid hope she had been given in the past two years.

Her feet were beginning to ache, and she was starting to consider nibbling the half-bun that was likely all she would eat today, when she spotted them: a knot of women sitting around near a fishing boat, perched on old crates, cleaning fish. Their chatter reached Chrissie's ears like a melody. She quickened her step, her heart thudding in her throat. The women looked happy, healthy, if poor. If Dovie was one of them, then perhaps she could work with them, and perhaps she could find Jonah again, and—

The woman right in front of her, sitting with her back to Chrissie, had curly hair. Just like Chrissie did. She was trembling slightly as she walked up to them, clutching the bag over her shoulder. Was her whole life about to change? A familiar despairing hope rushed through her veins, the hope that had let her down so many times, yet that she could not let go of.

She stopped a few feet away. A woman sitting across the circle from her looked up. "Are you all right, pet?" she asked.

Chrissie swallowed tears. She couldn't say a single word. She just stood there, shaking, until the curly-haired woman in front of her turned around, and she had a great hook nose and sharp features, nothing like Chrissie's own snub nose and round cheeks.

But Chrissie had to ask. She had to. "Do you know Dovie Brentcliff?" she croaked.

"Dovie?" said the curly-haired woman, and Chrissie's heart leaped.

But the woman shook her head slowly. "Sorry, dear. I don't."

"All right." Chrissie felt her body sink three inches, felt the breath leave her body as her hope was crushed for the thousandth time. "Thank you," she croaked, and turned to walk further into cold and heartless London, still completely alone.

AT LEAST THE sleeping place that Chrissie found was not the worst she'd ever had.

The worst she'd ever had was exposed on the sidewalk next to a busy street on the edge of the Old Nichol. Wheels had sprayed slush on her, a stray dog had nibbled at her hand while she slept, and three men had woken her up when they tried to steal her coat from her very body.

This was not as bad as the sidewalk near the Old Nichol, because at least she was mostly out of sight, tucked between some barrels on the docks. But the damp made it almost as bad. It seeped through the ground while she slept, chilling her deep inside her bones, so that when she woke up, her clothes clung to her skin as though she'd been sweating.

She sat up with a gasp. Her bag was clutched in her arms to keep it safe from street urchins, and she rummaged in it at once, her heart thudding when she felt the rag wrapped around Jonah's letters was damp. She unwrapped them, pulled them out, and breathed a sigh of relief. They were undamaged. She had already dried them carefully so many times after they'd been rained on that it was almost impossible to read the words.

Tears stung her eyes. If only she could tell Jonah where she was... if only she could receive a new letter from him. She kissed, gently, the one he had given her the last time she had seen or heard from him: in the village two years ago. There was no way of knowing whether he was dead or alive, whether he was getting her letters or not.

She tucked the letters away in her bag and got to her feet, ignoring her cold, sore joints that protested from sleeping on the cold, damp ground. Pushing out from among the barrels of fish, she dodged around the fishermen and ran into the crowded street before anyone could see her.

The long drudgery of her day began. She walked up to the first shop she saw; a fish-and-chip shop, with people emerging in droves, clutching greasy parcels wrapped in newspaper that smelled utterly heavenly. Chrissie couldn't remember the last time she'd had an entire piece of fried fish all to herself.

There was a wreath on the fish shop door, all bright holly and deep garland. Chrissie stared at it for a moment, remembering the wreaths she had made with Nana Beulah, and her heart squeezed in her chest. Pushing the door open, she strode into the little shop, filled with the sound of frying. She tried not to let the smells distract her, even though her stomach panged with hunger, and walked up to the counter with her best smile.

The woman behind the counter looked her up and down with a glare. "Ain't givin' nothin' away here, child. Go away."

"I'm not here to beg, ma'am," said Chrissie. "I'm looking for work. I used to manage the weaving room at a cotton mill, and I can read and write." She pushed the words out quickly, before the woman could interrupt her.

"Read and write?" the woman scoffed. "A street rat like you?"

"If you lend me a pencil, I'll show you," said Chrissie eagerly.

The woman glared at her. "No need. I won't hire no one who's a liar."

Chrissie had heard those words many, many times before, but they never lost their sting. "I'm not lying to you, ma'am."

"Yes, you are. Who hires a mere child like you—what are you? Thirteen? Fourteen?—to manage part of a cotton mill?" The woman snorted. "Now buy something or get out of my shop."

Even a tiny portion of chips was more expensive than Chrissie could afford. Head hanging, she stumbled out of the shop, looking around listlessly for her next opportunity. There was a gentleman on the street corner, and she approached him slowly, holding out a skinny hand.

"It's nearly Christmas, sir," she wheedled. "Spare a penny for the poor?"

The man looked her up and down and walked away quickly, as though he wanted to avoid her. As though poverty was catching. She crossed the street and stood on the corner in the path of a batch of young women, jolly creatures with ribbons in their hair, clutching brown paper parcels that looked like Christmas presents.

"Alms for the poor?" she whispered, holding out her cupped hands. "Alms for Christmas?"

The women's eyes slid over her as though she wasn't there, and Chrissie watched them go, her hands still outstretched out of habit, her eyes stinging with tears. She hated being invisible more than anything else in the world. Her eye caught a little slop-shop on the corner, and she took a deep breath, ready to walk toward it. Perhaps she would be luckier there and find a job as a slopworker.

Her heart felt as cold and empty as a cave in the snow. Last Christmas, she had lost the toe, and lay fevered in an alleyway for days, believing that it was the end. Would this Christmas be any different? She squeezed her eyes shut, her hands still held out in front of her, trying to hold back the tears. Things had been so different when she'd still had a family. She remembered looking forward to Christmas with bubbling joy; she remembered warm fires and a tree in the corner and roast chicken and oranges. But more than that, she remembered the way Nana Beulah and Papa Roy would look at her, with warm eyes and wide smiles. If only someone, anyone, would smile at her again.

She prayed, because prayer was the only thing that ever lifted her aching heart anymore. *Oh, Father, please... please let this time be different. Let this Christmas be the one where I find my mother... let this Christmas be different.*

Something cold and hard fell into her palm. She winced, tugging her hands back, then glanced down into them. A bright tuppence shimmered in her palm.

"Oh, thank you." Chrissie gasped, looking up.

The young man on the street corner tipped his hat to her as though she was a lady, even though his own coat was patched and faded. "It's nearly Christmas, isn't it?" He smiled, then turned to go on his way.

"Please, sir," Chrissie gasped. "Wait."

The young man stopped. "I haven't any more money. I'm sorry. I have to go to buy food for my little ones."

"No, sir, I wouldn't ask more of you. I... I just thought you might know someone I'm looking for. My mother," said Chrissie.

He paused. "Maybe I do. What's her name?"

"Dovie," said Chrissie. "Dovie Brentcliff. She looks just like me, but older."

The man was shaking his head before she finished speaking. "I'm sorry. I don't recognize your face, and I don't know anyone by that name, either."

Chrissie's shoulders sagged. "That's all right, sir. Thank you."

"I'm truly sorry," the young man said again. He paused. "Are you looking for work?"

"I am." Chrissie stepped forward. "I can read and write, sir. I used to work in a cotton mill. I managed part of it." She bit her lip. "I truly did."

The young man smiled. "I saw a sign outside the hotel just up the street. They're looking for someone to work for them." He shrugged. "Perhaps you can try them."

"Thank you. Oh, thank you, sir," Chrissie gasped.

"Merry Christmas," said the young man, and walked away. It was the first time anyone had said that to her in two years.

CHAPTER 13

THE HOTEL WAS WILDLY alight with Christmas. Wreaths hung on all of its shuttered windows; there was a huge one on the door, all wrapped in red ribbons and hung with tiny brass bells that tinkled merrily when Chrissie pushed the door open. When she stepped into the lobby, it was warmer and brighter than any place she had been since she had left the Wentworth house. The carpet was red and very deep, and a great, roaring fire leaped in the hearth.

She had stopped by a puddle to wash some of the grime out of her hair, even though the resultant chill had made her shiver. She could only pray that the effort was worth it; even as she strode up to the polished wooden counter at the end of the room, Chrissie could feel a tickle starting in the back of her throat.

She had already lost a toe last winter. She feared she might lose far more in this one if this didn't work. But she'd seen the sign in the window, HELP WANTED, in bold as though they were desperate. Perhaps even desperate enough to hire her.

The man behind the counter had frizzy hair that stuck up in all directions and dark circles under his eyes. He barely glanced up at her as she came in. "Our rooms are a shilling per night. I doubt you can afford it. Please leave."

"Are you in need of help, sir?" Chrissie asked.

The man stared at her. "I need someone who can read and write. I can't employ ragamuffins who are illiterate."

"I can read and write," said Chrissie quickly. "I can show you, if you wish."

The man stared at her, his eyes narrowing. "Very well. Spell the word 'Christmas'."

Chrissie hid her smile. She'd been able to spell her own name since she was five years old. "C-H-R-I-S-T-M-A-S," she said, then turned to point at the poster on the wall over the lobby. "No dogs allowed in the rooms."

The man stared at her. "Sixpence a week," he said at last, "and you'll have a uniform and a small room. That's all. Take it or leave it."

Chrissie's heart flipped over. Was it truly as simple as that? The relief that rushed through her veins was fierce and intense. "Sir, that would be wonderful," she gasped.

"You will work every day. You may rest from one to five on Sunday afternoons—you'll work Sunday nights. Understood?" the man barked.

"Yes, sir. Thank you, sir. Thank you." Chrissie sobbed out the words. "Thank you."

She had expected the heavens to open, angels to sing over this Christmas miracle in her life. Instead, the man reached under the counter and pulled out a black-and-white maid's uniform and a rusty key on a piece of string. "Servants' quarters are down that hallway, to the right. You'll have room number four. Get yourself dressed and report to the head housekeeper. Then get to work. And don't think you'll be getting any of your money in advance, either. You'll be paid at the end of the week like everybody else."

"Yes, sir. Thank you, sir." Chrissie gushed, clutching the uniform in her hands, careful not to let it touch the front of her grubby dress.

The man waved an irritable hand. "Get out of the lobby. You're too scruffy to be seen like this. For heaven's sake, try to neaten yourself up."

Chrissie bolted down the hallway, tears of gratitude flowing down her cheeks. There would be no missing toes or fevers for her this Christmas, and that in itself was a gift.

⚜

THE MERRY PIANO music filled the hotel, even reaching up to the third floor, where Chrissie was on her hands and knees, scrubbing out a bath.

Their latest guests had arrived last night—Christmas Eve—and Chrissie had no idea where they'd come from, but they seemed to have brought all the road dust of England with them. The white porcelain bath was covered in a nasty brown film, and some of it stuck to her fingers, cold and slimy, while she scrubbed. Her knees hurt from the pressure on the cold floor, but she smiled as she worked, knowing where her next meal was coming from, knowing where she was going to sleep tonight even if it snowed, and listening to the Christmas carol rising up through the floorboards.

She could only dimly make out the words as all the guests sang together, some of them a little worse for wear after the many glasses of eggnog that Chrissie's colleagues were carrying all around the party on silver trays, but the joyous piano tune was enough to take her memory back to warmer days when she would dress up in her nicest clothes with the other children and walk the streets of the village, singing.

Led by the light of Faith serenely beaming

With glowing hearts by His cradle we stand.

It was Nana Beulah's favorite Christmas carol. Chrissie swallowed a few tears at the thought as she scrubbed out the last of the bath and gave it a wipe down with a cloth. It was shining white by the time she got up off her knees, stretching her aching back, and smoothed down the front of her uniform. The work was hard, but it didn't matter. All that mattered was that she felt a little safer now.

And that, come the end of the week, she would have the money to send a letter to Jonah again. Maybe she would even tell him she had a new job, that he could write to the hotel, and maybe he would respond, and she would read his letters again at last...

No. Chrissie shook her head to herself as she gathered up her cleaning things. She couldn't admit to Jonah how she had suffered in the past few years; as far as he knew, she was still working at the cotton mill. Jonah would never forgive himself if he thought that Chrissie had gotten thrown onto the streets because she had gone to visit him.

There was another, more fearful motive deep in Chrissie's heart as she packed the last of her cleaning things into a basket. If she couldn't get Jonah's letters, she could tell herself that he was all right. That he was safe and happy in the village, that his siblings had found work again, that his mother had gotten better. If she didn't know how he was, she could ignore the little voice in the back of her mind that told her that if all was well with Jonah, he would long since have come looking for her.

She pushed the niggling thought away and skimmed the scrap of paper on which the head housekeeper had written her list of afternoon chores. *When finished, meet me in the kitchen.* Chrissie stuffed the note in her pocket and hurried downstairs.

The kitchen was quiet now, its pots and pans resting on the stove, its shelves empty of dishes. The head housekeeper sat at the kitchen table, reading. She looked up as Chrissie came in. "Ah, yes. Christmas. Were you able to get that bath cleaned?"

"Silvery white again, ma'am," said Chrissie.

"Good girl. Well, the meal's been served, and it'll be a while before the dishes have to be washed again. It's going to be a long night for everyone; the party won't be finished until midnight at the earliest, and then we'll have to go in and clean up the hall. Why don't you go to your room and have a minute's rest?" said the housekeeper. "Come back at once when you hear the bell ring."

"Thank you, ma'am. I will." Chrissie nodded to the house-keeper and scurried away to her room. The room was little more than a cubicle, barely long enough for the door to swing open without knocking into the little trunk at the foot of the bed, and barely wide enough for Chrissie to move along the side of her bed so that she could get in. She shut the door and scrambled onto the foot of the bed, opening the trunk and pulling out the only treasures she owned: Jonah's letters, and a scrap of notepaper and a stub of pencil, which the housekeeper had thrown away because the paper was a little stained. Chrissie had fished them out of the rubbish at once.

She lit a candle and lay on her belly on the bed, propping the paper against the lid of the trunk, listening. They were playing a different carol now; she couldn't quite hear which one, since her quarters were so far from the party. Part of her wished to be in that bright room with the guests, eating the feast she'd helped to prepare, the potatoes she'd peeled, from the dishes she washed, but right now all the Christmas she needed was the promise of a letter she could post to Jonah in a few days when the post office opened again.

Dear Jonah, she wrote.

It's a lovely Christmas here. Very cold, but I can hear a Christmas carol being sung, and it's beautiful. I wish you were here with me—or that I was there with you.

She thought of the loft of Farmer Green's barn and wondered if things would have been different if she'd stayed. Maybe she would have found work in the village, after all; it had taken her two years to get work here in the city. Surely the village could have been no worse? She sighed. The difference was that she would have been a burden on Jonah, a thought she couldn't bear.

Do you remember the fairy tale we used to tell each other about how Princess Chrissie and Prince Jonah would rescue the Snowflake Queen from the land of shadows? I think about that all the time. I miss you, Prince Jonah.

I can't wait to see you again, someday very soon. I hope you're very well.

Love,

Chrissie.

She finished the letter and lay back on the bed, watching the candlelight cast shadows on the ceiling. And even though things were so much better, even though she had food and a room to sleep in and a real bed again for the first time in years, Chrissie's heart still throbbed with a great hollow space where Jonah should be.

PART VI

CHAPTER 14

Two Years Later

JONAH WHISTLED to himself as he worked, trying to take his mind off the bitter cold that made his fingers numb and made it all the more difficult to force the big needle through the leather and rubber. He grunted with effort, hauling the thick waxed thread through the shoe, then turned the needle around and did it again. His fingers and thumbs were already hard and callused from the word, and the cold made them clumsy, but Jonah's brows knotted in concentration, and he made every stitch exactly even.

"Let me see your work, boy," growled the old cobbler.

Jonah looked up at him. Mr. Simpson had a voice like a box of rocks being shaken, and he glared at Jonah out of one eye, the other permanently half-shut. His hands, ruined with decades of making and repairing shoes, were gnarled and almost useless.

"Yes, sir." Jonah handed over the half-finished shoe, the needle still dangling from its thread below it. It was a farmer's boot, the leather worn and patched already, and the new sole was half sewn on. Mr. Simpson turned it over in his hands a few times, then grunted. "It'll do." He handed it back and shuffled off to go to the shopfront and talk to customers.

Jonah smiled to himself. That was high praise coming from Mr. Simpson. He went back to sewing, trying not to think of Farmer Green's boots, which had looked just like this.

Mr. Simpson came shuffling into the room again and perched on a three-legged stool in front of the fire, holding his hands out to the flames. "That was Mrs. Paxton picking up her shoes."

"I hope she likes them," said Jonah.

Mr. Simpson grunted. "She wouldn't have paid for them if she didn't like them."

Jonah said nothing, continuing with his work, but he couldn't help whistling softly between his teeth. Mr. Simpson glowered at him from the stool, trying to warm his old bones. "What are you whistling Christmas carols for, boy? It's barely December."

"I love Christmas, sir," said Jonah.

"Fool," growled Mr. Simpson. "Your mother died on Christmas, didn't she?"

"Yes, sir." Jonah nodded. "And Farmer Green just a few days after." It was the destruction of his world in one fell swoop.

"And you spent nearly a week on the street," Mr. Simpson grumbled. "Siblings all packed off to relatives in Scotland who didn't want you because you were too old."

"Yes, sir," said Jonah.

"It must have been the worst time of your life, boy. So why love it?" Mr. Simpson demanded.

Not for the first time, Jonah wondered about Mrs. Simpson. People spoke of her, but never Mr. Simpson. They said she, too, had died in the winter.

"Because the person I love most in the whole world was born around Christmastime, and she always loved it," said Jonah.

Mr. Simpson huffed. "Love is as foolish as Christmas is." He wrapped his bony arms around himself and glowered into the flames.

Perhaps it was, but on cold days like these, Jonah couldn't stop thinking about Chrissie's letters. They had been coming much more frequently for the past two years. Though, she wrote to his old address, and he had to fetch the letters when he could. Still, she must have been given a promotion at the cotton mill, Jonah thought, to have more money to buy stamps so regular like; but he didn't know. She never talked about her work in her letters. In fact, she never talked about anything Jonah told her, either, or even commented on the fact that he'd been quiet for six months after his mother had died. She hadn't expressed her sympathy after Mama's passing. But she always wrote about how she loved him and missed him, and about all their good times together as children, so surely, she still cared? She must be trying to distract him from his troubles by not writing about them.

Jonah didn't know, but as he worked, he thought of the tiny pouch of coins lying under the straw mattress in the cellar where he slept. Mr. Simpson didn't pay him much, not once he'd been fed, but it was enough that he could tuck a few pennies away every now and then. Pennies that would ultimately fulfil his promise to Chrissie: that he would come to find her. The thought made his heart thump hard. Only another week or so. Soon, *soon*, he would hold her in his arms again.

He whistled a few more bars of the Christmas carol. "O Holy Night", Chrissie's favorite.

CHRISSIE GAVE the brass taps in the washroom a last polish with her cloth and stepped back, looking around the big room. It was sparkling with cleanliness, ready for the next guests to arrive tonight, and she couldn't help smiling with satisfaction. In a matter of days, the hotel would begin bursting at the seams as people poured to London from all over England to spend Christmas with their relatives, and soon there wouldn't be time to step back and admire her work anymore.

She picked up her basket and headed downstairs to the kitchen. At least she would still have her half-day off every Sunday, even if she would have to work all of Christmas Eve and all of Christmas Day, as usual. There would be time for a letter to Jonah, perhaps. Her heart squeezed, and she thought again that she should give him her new address... But no. It was easier this way, to not know. Because every time she thought of giving him her address, she thought of his mother being ill and how afraid he was that it might be catching, and she thought of the smallpox that had taken Joe Wilkes, and she feared that if she told Jonah where she was, she might find out that she had been writing to a phantom all this time.

She pushed the thought aside as she stepped into the kitchen, already fragrant with the roast that was browning slowly in the oven. "I'm all done with my list, Mrs. Towers," she said.

"Good girl." Mrs. Towers was bent over a ledger at the kitchen table, writing. "Have your cup of tea quickly now, then go on with the dining hall."

"Yes, ma'am." Chrissie obediently headed into the servants' hall, which bustled with conversation while the maids and bellhops helped themselves to cups of tea and biscuits in a fifteen-minute break before the afternoon chaos began.

She poured herself a cup of tea, longing for the milk and sugar that Nana Beulah always used to put in it and took a tasteless biscuit before sliding into an empty chair beside Jamie Frank, one of the bellhops.

"How was your morning, Jamie?" Chrissie asked. "Are those new people nice?"

"Nice enough, I suppose," said Jamie, "for a Monday." He gave her a rakish grin.

Jill Price, the maid who always batted her eyelashes at Jamie, was sitting next to him. She elbowed him in the ribs. "Tell her, Jamie."

"About what?" Chrissie asked.

"Oh." Jamie's eyes widened. "You know how you've asked us to keep an ear open for someone called Dovie Brentcliff?"

Hearing someone else say her mother's name made Chrissie's heart stutter in her chest. Every Sunday afternoon, she had been combing the city for Dovie, asking and asking everyone she saw if they knew her. Everyone shook their heads. But now Jamie was actually saying her name as though she was a real person, someone that Chrissie might just find, eventually. Someone who might be her Christmas miracle.

"Have you heard of her?" Chrissie asked eagerly.

"Well, I don't know about Brentcliff, but in the pub yesterday someone mentioned a woman named Dovie," said Jamie.

Chrissie clutched her teacup in a shaking hand. It wasn't a common name. "Did they say where?"

"I asked *them*, although it did my reputation no good." Jamie winced. "Before I tell you, Chrissie, there's something you should know."

The look in his eyes made a cold wind blow through Chrissie's heart. "Is she... dead?" she whispered.

"What? No—not dead. Perhaps worse." Jamie leaned closer to her, glancing around, and whispered the words. "She's— working on the streets."

Chrissie sat back with a jolt. Jonah had been right. The thought sent a flood of disappointment through her, but it couldn't eclipse her joy at hearing her mother's name. "Did they say where she is?" she pressed.

Jonah sighed. "Yes. She was on the corner of Pine and Bauble Streets. But you can't go there, Chrissie. It's terribly danger-ous. Certainly, don't go alone. It's no place for a pretty girl like you."

At that, Jill gasped in shock at Jamie calling Chrissie pretty, and they were soon too caught up in their lover's quarrel to notice how much Chrissie was shaking. She didn't care if

Dovie worked the streets. She didn't care if it was dangerous.

She needed a family, and if Dovie was all there was for her, then Dovie would have to do.

❦

JONAH'S HEART pounded with excitement. He leaned against the stagecoach window, looking around at the enormous buildings that towered against the sky. Never in his life had he seen such vast buildings before. They could swallow up the whole church back in the village.

But he was a long way from the village now, and as the stage-coach bumped to a halt at the crossroads, Jonah tumbled out into a freezing day. The sky was slate grey above him, and even though there was no snow lying on the streets right now, he was certain that there would be, before very long. The air tasted smoky and bitter; everywhere he looked, chimneys belched vapours into the sky.

So this was the great city of London. He'd been expecting more.

He turned back to the stagecoach driver. "You'll be here at six o' clock, you said?"

The driver nodded. "Don't be late," he grunted, and turned to attend to the new horses being hitched to the coach.

Jonah had written enough letters to Dovie that he knew her address by heart. The driver had told him to just go down this street until he saw Star Road; it was the only cotton mill on that road. The rest of the buildings were match factories. Jonah had heard stories about the match factories, and he could only be grateful Chrissie worked in the mill instead.

Maybe not forever, though. He set off down the road with quick steps, his heart filled with excited dreams. Today, he would see Chrissie again at last for the first time in four long years. He would wrap her in his arms and tell her how their childhood friendship had blossomed into fierce love. He would tell her he was going to come to get her, to take her away from this city to a place where the grass was green in summer and the snow was white in winter. Today might not be that day—but at least he could visit her more often. At least their love would be allowed to grow into something.

And he would ask her why she never reacted to the things he wrote about. The thought furrowed his brow, but he pushed it away. She would have an explanation. She would be doing it out of love. Jonah's Chrissie only ever did anything out of love.

The squalor appalled him as he headed down the street. He had never seen anything like this before: the piles of garbage lying in the street, the bony men and women staring at him from the shadows of dark alleyways, the bony stray dogs that picked their way through the rubbish and raised their hackles when Jonah even looked at them. He had never smelled anything worse than that city. It was an acrid, chemical stench, and he already longed to go back to the village.

At last, Star Road, lined with ugly, squat buildings, and Jonah spotted a wagon loaded with bales of fabric clattering out from behind one of them. That had to be the factory. He walked up to a small door at the front and knocked.

"Enter," barked a voice from within.

Jonah took a deep breath. He prayed that he wasn't going to upset Bertram Jones by looking for Chrissie. Pushing the door open, he stepped into a tiny, cluttered office. An ugly man with protruding eyes and huge front teeth sat hunched over his desk, and he glared at Jonah's rags as soon as he saw him.

"What do you want? I don't have work for you. Go away," he barked.

"I'm not here looking for work, sir," said Jonah. "I'm looking for someone."

"Who?" Bertram snapped.

Jonah squared his shoulders. "Christmas Ellis."

Bertram's eyes narrowed. "She's not here."

Jonah felt a breath of terrible cold rush through his body. "Not here? But... but she works here."

"She used to," snapped Bertram, "until four years ago, when the little fool disappeared for three days over Christmas. Now she's gone."

"Gone?" cried Jonah. "Gone where?"

"I don't know, and I don't care. Now go away before I *make* you go," snapped Bertram.

Jonah stumbled out of the office, his heart thundering. Four years ago, Chrissie had come to visit him. And as a result, Bertram and Chloe had thrown her out onto the streets.

Now she was gone, and he had no idea where to find her.

Why hadn't she told him? How could she do this? It would be months, now, before he could scrounge together the money to find her again. Tears stung his eyes as he walked down the street. It was just beginning to snow, heavy, damp flakes that melted as soon as they landed on Jonah's shoulders, soaking him with water.

He would see nothing of Chrissie this Christmas. He didn't know where she was or if she was all right.

And it made him feel more alone than ever before.

CHAPTER 15

PINE AND BAUBLE Streets were in the Old Nichol.

Chrissie kept her hands tucked tightly into the pockets of her coat as she walked down Pine Street, trying her best to avoid the puddles of filth that lay everywhere. It had snowed yesterday, but that snow had already been turned into slush, and the slush had been churned into mud here, where the streets had no paving at all. Mud sucked at her shoes, soaking into them until her feet were freezing and sodden.

She skirted around a puddle with an unhealthy layer of shimmering oil on the top, maybe from a dead rat that lay half-in and half-out of the water, its ugly yellow teeth jutting out. This led her almost into the path of a ragged child sitting on the street, a row of cigarette butts lined up on a scrap of paper in front of her. Chrissie nearly knocked into one of the cigarette butts, and the child shook her fist, yelling out a filthy curse.

Chrissie sucked in a nervous breath and tucked a strand of her hair behind her ear. This place was just an hour's walk from the hotel, but it felt as though it belonged in another, far more hostile world.

Her heart thumped when she saw the signpost just up ahead. Bauble Street. Jamie had seen Dovie here, on this very street corner. Her step quickened, and she hurried forward onto the crossroads, looking eagerly left and right.

But there was nothing here. No one but a sullen-eyed man pushing a rotten, rickety handcart across the mud. Nothing but a sagging fence made of rusty wire and leaning sticks for fence posts, containing a donkey whose ribs jutted out like barrel hoops. Even the building across the street, its hand painted sign reading simply PUB, was still and empty.

Chrissie's shoulders sagged. Yet again, Dovie wasn't here.

She turned to the ragged man with the handcart. "Excuse me, sir?"

The man gave her a listless look out of yellow eyes. "This is no place for you, missy. Go home."

"I'm looking for a lady named Dovie Brentcliff. She was here a few nights ago," said Chrissie. "Did you see her?"

The man's lips turned down at the corners.

"I wouldn't call her a *lady*. She won't be here during the day," he sneered, and rumbled off with his handcart.

Chrissie's hands closed into fists. Dovie's trail had not yet gone completely cold.

❦

THE OLD NICHOL had been terrifying enough during the day. At night, it was worse than a nightmare.

Chrissie took short, terrified breaths as she jogged along the street, hurrying for the corner of Pine and Bauble. The dilapidated buildings that had looked so forlorn and sorrowful in daylight loomed above her now, only their sketchy silhouettes visible in the dim light of the occasional watery streetlamp, their leaning walls and half-collapsed roofs giving them twisted and monstrous shapes as though they could come alive at any moment, pounce, and devour her.

The danger of the houses was imagined. But Chrissie knew, deep in her bones, that the other dangers of this street were very, very real.

She ignored the squelching of her feet in the deep, noisome mud, even when her lost toe began to shoot phantom pains up her ankle. Losing a toe was the least of her concerns right now.

Two days had passed since Sunday afternoon, when Chrissie had first come looking for Dovie here. It had taken her that long both to pluck up her courage to venture out at night, and to make a plan to slip out of the hotel unseen. It was only thanks to a late-night carouser at the hotel bar that she had been able to sneak outside while the bellhops were focused on getting the drunken gentleman to his room in one piece.

How she was going to get back in, she didn't know. All that would have to wait for after she found Dovie.

A burst of laughter to her left made her jump, whipping around, seeing the wild leap of firelight. Some men had made a low, smoky fire in a hollowed-out house, blackened and gutted by some tragedy. They sat around it, swigging from little black bottles that shone expensively in the firelight even though their clothes hung in tatters from their bodies, showing glimpses of naked, shrunken flesh. Others lay on the floor around them, their eyes distant and wild, muttering in their opium-riddled half-reality.

Chrissie shivered and hurried on, relieved they hadn't seen her. She was suddenly and acutely aware of her tumbling curls and the way even her cheap cotton dress so easily hugged her hips and chest, filled out now by approaching womanhood.

Bauble Street wasn't far now. Soon, she'd look into her mother's eyes for the first time since the night she was born. Soon, she would—

An iron fist gripped her elbow. "Hello there," hissed a voice, its reeking breath huffing in her face.

Chrissie whipped around, ripping her arm from her captor's grip. She stumbled backward into the street, her heart fluttering wildly in her throat, as two boys emerged from the shadows of a doorway. They were both skinny; one tall and stooped, one short, both of them with the same wild, hungry look in their eyes. The same look as that in the eyes of the stray dogs that picked through the rubbish at the back of the hotel.

"I'm in a hurry." She backed away faster.

One of the boys made a grab for her. Chrissie just barely dodged it.

"We're not," chuckled the shorter boy.

"Anyone ever told you how very pretty you are?" murmured the taller one.

She kept backing away, and they just kept coming. Her heart seemed to be beating in all the wrong places.

"Such lovely hair." The shorter one made a grab for it, and one lock slid between his grimy fingers before Chrissie pulled it away.

"Oh, the hair's nothing." The taller one gave a throaty chuckle, his eyes traveling up and down her body.

"Please," Chrissie choked. "I'm—I'm on my way somewhere." Her back slammed into a wall with a thump, and she realized that she had reached the other side of the street.

"Oh, no," said the taller boy, his voice softly menacing, his eyes roving her body. "Not anymore, you aren't."

He reached out, and panic gripped her. With a speed she hadn't known she possessed, Chrissie ducked under his outstretched arm and bolted down the street, her feet frantic in the mud, spraying filth from the puddles with every stride. She heard laughter behind her, slapping footsteps, knew they were chasing her, and fled with the speed of a hare in flight from a pack of hungry, slavering dogs.

Chrissie had no idea how long she spent running, but she knew that even when it felt as though her heart and lungs would burst, even when her legs were afire and her feet had gone numb with cold and wet, she pushed herself faster and faster still. She did not look back. She did not listen for the boys. She simply ran the whole way, jogging here and there when her body felt that it would burst, until she was slipping through the back door of the hotel again, weeping with relief that forgetful Jamie had left it unlocked, until she had sprinted up the steps and thrown herself into her bed and pulled her covers over her head. And when she had pulled her pillow over her face, she wept until sleep came for her at last.

"DID you go looking for Dovie last night?"

Jamie hissed the words during breakfast, leaning close to Chrissie despite the furious glare that Jill gave them both. She jumped, stared up at him with eyes that felt like they'd been filled with sand, and then quickly ducked her head over her tasteless porridge.

"Please," she whispered, terrified, "don't tell Mrs. Towers."

"I won't," said Jamie softly, "but you know you should never go there, Chrissie. You're lucky you weren't killed—or worse."

Chrissie took another spoonful of the porridge, shuddering down the length of her body. Jamie had no idea how close she had come to a terrible fate.

"It's too dangerous. Don't go there again—please," said Jamie.

Chrissie blinked back her tears. Last night, when she'd been running home with all of her strength, she'd promised herself that she would never go back again. But just this morning, earlier, when the guests had been eating breakfast in the hotel dining hall, she had paused to peer through the half-open door. She'd seen a little girl sitting beside her mother, giggling while her mother cut her toast into soldiers, and a fresh pang of longing had filled her heart.

"You can't go back there." Jamie's eyes widened at the look on her face.

"I have to." Chrissie took another mouthful of porridge. "I just do."

Jamie stared at her. "I wish I'd never told you about Dovie."

"She's my mother, Jamie," Chrissie hissed. "I've never met her, but she's my mother and I want to find her. I *have* to find her. She's the only family I have left." Except for her grandparents, she supposed, whoever they were; Nana and Papa almost never spoke of them.

Jamie sighed. "I won't go with you, Chrissie. It's asking to get yourself dismissed. And I can't go back onto the streets again."

Chrissie stared down into the grey gunk in her bowl. She couldn't go back, either, but neither could she continue to lead this lonely, loveless existence.

"I'm going," she murmured.

Jamie shook his head. "Tonight?"

"Yes."

"Then I'll leave my coat by the back door for you. It's big enough that you should look different wearing it. And for Pete's sake, cover your head." He huffed a sigh. "I'll leave the back door unlocked for you again."

Chrissie stared at him, relief rushing through her. "Thank you."

"What are you whispering about?" Jill demanded loudly.

"Nothing." Jamie straightened, giving her a winning smile. "Why, Jill, your hair does look lovely today."

Jill giggled, and Chrissie tackled the rest of her breakfast with renewed determination. This time, she would find Dovie.

AND THIS TIME, she did.

There were many times, on her way down the long, long Pine Street, that Chrissie realized she was mad to do this, and knew she should turn back. But she didn't. She couldn't resign herself to another lonely Christmas, belonging to no one and mattering to nobody. The thought of that was even worse than the watchful eyes of every man she passed, but thanks to Jamie's baggy overcoat with its hood pulled well over her face and hair, none of them spoke to her. None of them even looked twice.

And when she reached the corner of Pine and Bauble, she spotted her at once.

Seeing Dovie was like looking into the small mirror over the cold washbasin all the female staff shared in the hotel. She looked old, of course, her cheeks thin and pale and embattled, her eyes very red, and she wore face paint that failed to cover her unhealthy grey pallor. Her lips were painted brightest red; her cheeks rouged to almost the same shade, and there were blue shadows around her eyes. She wore a tattered dress that plunged scandalously low in the front and didn't seem shy about turning to every man who passed, just like the other women on the corner with her. But despite all these differences, Chrissie's heart knew at once that this was her mother. She looked so much like Chrissie in every other way—in the shape of her face and body, in the shade of her eyes and hair.

She reminded her of Nana Beulah, and that fact made Chrissie stand very still across the street for a few long seconds, taking deep breaths to swallow her tears. She had found someone else in the world who had Nana Beulah's blood flowing through their veins.

She had found *family*, for the first time in the seven years since Papa Roy had died.

Her feet somehow carried her across the street, her singing heart lifting her so that she almost floated up to the women. She knew that happy tears were rushing down her cheeks and that she couldn't stop the wide smile spreading across her face.

"Dovie?" she gasped. "It's you, isn't it? It's really you."

Dovie turned around, and the eyes that found Chrissie's were eerily the same shade as her own. They widened.

"Who's this, Dovie?" asked one of the other women. "She's your spitting image."

"No one," Dovie barked. Her voice was harsh and gravely, worn by smoking, and Chrissie blinked at the sound of it. It was nothing like her own.

"It's me," said Chrissie. "Christmas. Your little girl."

"Hush," Dovie hissed. She glanced back at the other women, then grabbed Chrissie's arm in a cold, thin hand and dragged her a few doors down, ducking into a narrow alleyway between two shops. "What are you playing at, coming here?"

"I wanted to find you." Chrissie felt a great crack running through her dreams of having a family this Christmas. "I wanted... I wanted to meet my mother."

Dovie looked away, wrapping her bony arms around her fragile body. "I never asked to be your mother."

Chrissie blinked, tears stinging her eyes. "I don't understand."

Dovie huffed. "You're not missing out on anything, girl. Trust me. You're better off without a mother." Her eyes hardened. "I know I'm better off without mine."

Chrissie's heart was spilling over with questions. "What's she like?" she managed. "My grandma. Who is she?"

"The one who destroyed my life," Dovie snapped. "I was almost an heiress, do you know that? I had suitors. I had a *ballgown*." She tugged at her ragged dress. "Until your grandmother decided I wasn't good enough for her anymore."

"Hey, Dovie," one of the other ladies of the night called.

Dovie waved an irritable hand at her, turning back to Chrissie. Her eyes were contemplative; Chrissie realized that the front of Jamie's ugly coat had blown open. "You're pretty," Dovie said. It wasn't a compliment.

Chrissie ignored it. "I... I don't want to be any trouble. I have a good job. I just want to know you... maybe to spend Christmas with you." Her eyes filled with tears. "I just want to know my mama."

"You don't have one. You never have," Dovie spat. "But you could have a good colleague, if you wanted."

"A colleague? What do you mean?" Chrissie asked.

"Syphilis took the last girl." Dovie shrugged. "We need more. Join the business with me. It's not as bad as you think it is, and you'll get money. And a safe place to sleep."

An appalling shudder ran down Chrissie's spine. She took a stumbling step back. "What? You want me to become—" She stopped.

Dovie's eyes turned hard. "Judgment from my own daughter." She spat on the mud near Chrissie's feet. "That's why I never want a family."

"Dovie, wait." Chrissie gasped.

Dovie didn't look back. "Go find your grandmother, Carol Brentcliff. She's as judgmental as you are. You'd like each other."

"I'm not judging you." Chrissie stumbled after her. "Dovie, *please*."

Dovie whirled around. With a harsh step forward, she slammed both hands into Chrissie's shoulders, sending her reeling backward so that she fell into the mud with a cry of pain and fright.

"I never wanted you," Dovie sneered. "And I never want to see you again."

She walked away to rejoin the other women. Chrissie dragged herself to her feet, pulling her coat closed around her, and fled, sobbing, tears streaming down her cheeks.

CHAPTER 16

DEAR JONAH,

You were right about Dovie. I should never have gone looking for her.

Chrissie stared down at the words on the page in the flickering candlelight. She sat in the kitchen, sipping a cup of tea at ten o' clock at night, waiting for the last guests to leave the dining hall so that she could start the arduous process of cleaning it. Her heart felt like a cannonball in her chest as she reread those words.

The memory of Dovie's face, of her cutting words, made tears prickle in Chrissie's eyes. *I never wanted you.* She bit her lip, blinking hard. Nana Beulah had told her that she was a princess in God's eyes. Jonah had always called her Princess Chrissie. But if the woman who had given birth to her, who had brought her into the world, if *she* thought Chrissie should never have existed, how could Nana and Jonah be right?

Something else about her conversation with Dovie rubbed at the corners of her mind. Her grandmother's name: Carol Brentcliff. Something about it seemed so familiar. She couldn't understand why.

The kitchen door opened, and Mrs. Towers peered inside. "The footmen are just clearing away the last of the plates now, Chrissie. Finish your tea and come to the dining hall."

"Yes, ma'am." Chrissie nodded and took a quick sip of her tea. She picked up her paper and pencil and pulled open the kitchen drawer, tucking them quickly away, and that was when she spotted the name.

Carol Brentcliff.

Chrissie's heart froze. She set the almost-finished tea down on the cabinet and pulled the drawer open a little wider. Mrs. Towers kept stacks of old newspapers in here for cleaning the grate, and there was one on the very top.

BRENTCLIFFS DONATE TO LOCAL ORPHANAGE, a headline blared.

Chrissie gasped. She remembered this article; she had so excitedly grabbed it and read it when the paper had first been delivered two weeks ago, remembering that her mother was called Dovie Brentcliff. But it was just a short snippet about some rich people who'd given money to an orphanage nearby.

Chrissie had decided that it had to be a coincidence. Whoever Dovie was, she certainly couldn't have rich parents.

I had suitors, Dovie had told her. Dovie *did* have rich parents. The people in this newspaper piece could be Chrissie's grandparents. And there it was, the name in the very first sentence:

Floyd and Carol Brentcliff, in anticipation of the upcoming Christmas season, generously donated...

Chrissie's heart thundered. There was an address in the article.

She had found her grandmother, just like that. And maybe this really was her Christmas miracle.

❦

CHRISSIE TREMBLED as she trudged up the long footpath to the Brentcliff house. She had spent a few precious coins getting an omnibus to take her as far as the edge of London; the driver had pointed out the towering house on the hilltop as belonging to the Brentcliffs. Chrissie could hardly believe it as she plodded up the hill. The tall wrought-iron gates were grand enough on their own. The house itself had turrets and columns and endless windows and a huge yard in the front with a fountain in the middle, even though it was frozen over now. And there was a living pine tree, towering and vast, in the center of the lawn, all hung with snow-dusted bows and enormous bright baubles, ready for Christmas.

Chrissie didn't go up the paved road to the wrought-iron gates. Instead, she took the rutted, muddy track that led around the back of the house, through an ordinary old gate, and up to the stable yard. Curious horses looked at her over their stable doors as she walked between them to the narrow door set in the back of the house. To her surprise, unlike the servants' entrance of the hotel, this door had a small wreath hanging on it.

She knocked, her heart thumping. It took several minutes before the door swung open, and a butler—a real butler with a starched white collar and a beautiful black tailcoat—looked down his long, hooked nose at her. "We have no work positions available. Kindly leave," he purred, and stepped aside to close the door.

"Wait. No," Chrissie cried, grabbing the door.

The butler glared at her.

"Sorry, sir. I'm sorry. I'm not looking for work." She held up both hands. "Please, just hear me out."

The butler's groomed veneer slipped sharply. "Why should I listen to an urchin like you? Go away." He began to close the door again.

"I'm Christmas Ellis." Chrissie cried. "Dovie's daughter. I'm Carol and Floyd's granddaughter."

Her outburst, at least, made the butler freeze in place. His eyes skimmed over her, and for a moment, they were thoughtful. Hope leaped in her. Then he shook his head. "What a ridiculous claim. My master and mistress will not tolerate such nonsense. Good day."

He slammed the door, and Christmas was left standing in the stable yard, shivering in the thin wind that howled across the yard. Misery rose in her like nausea. She pressed her hand into her pocket, feeling the few coins that lay there, just enough to get her home by omnibus by five o' clock to spend her Sunday night cleaning the hotel all alone. They were her life savings, and she had just wasted them.

She turned away and plodded across the stable yard, her arms wrapped around her body. She would finish her letter to Jonah tonight, and that would make her feel better... but of course, she never got any letters in return. Besides, Jonah was dead, she knew. She had always feared it, and now she believed it. Jonah was dead, Nana and Papa were dead. Dovie didn't want her, and neither did her grandparents.

Chrissie was alone. She would never have a family. Her Christmases would always be alone and empty and meaningless, and it was time to stop dreaming. It was time to stop believing in a time of hope and joy.

It was time to stop believing in princesses.

She didn't cry as she left the yard behind and started for the gate. What use was it? It was time for her heart to freeze over, like London's earth. Only there would be no spring and summer for her. Her heart would never bloom and bear wild-flowers of love again.

She had nearly reached the gate, more heartbroken and depressed than she had ever been in her life, when a voice floated through the windy day toward her. "Wait—wait!"

Chrissie stopped, turning back, in time to see a middle-aged woman scampering across the snow toward her, clutching at her thick skirts, her shoes sliding on the frozen ground.

"Wait!" the woman cried out again.

Chrissie stared at her, her hands hanging limp and useless by her sides. She didn't care what this woman wanted. She didn't care about anything.

"You—you said you were Dovie's child," the woman panted.

Chrissie nodded. "I am."

"Then don't go." The woman clutched at her hand. "I'm the housekeeper here. I knew Dovie, and I know you're telling the truth. You look just as she did when she—when she left." The woman's eyes filled with tears.

"You knew my mother?" Chrissie's heart thumped, though she did her best not to hope. "Why did she leave? Why did she leave *me*?"

"Dovie left because your grandmother told her to go." The housekeeper sighed. "When she heard that Dovie was going to have a baby though she wasn't married, she wanted nothing to do with the scandal, and so she cast her out into the world."

Chrissie's shoulders slumped. She knew she shouldn't have hoped. "So she won't want me, either."

"No. No. I don't think that's true." The housekeeper squeezed her hands. "Mrs. Brentcliff changed after they cast Dovie away. It shattered her. For ten years, she was bedridden, her nerves destroyed. The doctors thought she was dying of a broken heart. But she rose again, and ever since then, I know she's felt guilty over Dovie. She gives money away, treats her servants better than anyone else, even rescues dogs from the streets."

Chrissie thought of the article in the paper, about her grandparents giving money to the orphanage. "Will they accept me?" she breathed.

"I can't say for sure," said the housekeeper. "But I think you should try. You'll never get past old Thwaite, though—the butler. He's far too strait-laced for that." She bit her lip. "But he has to go into town tomorrow for an appointment; the mistress is generous with leave for that sort of thing. I'll be here alone. I can get you in to speak to your grandparents."

Chrissie's heart was truly pounding now, and even if she tried to stop it, hope was pouring through her, rich and golden. "Oh, please, please. But—tomorrow? It's Monday. I work at a hotel. They'll never let me go."

"They'll have to," said the housekeeper. "I'm leaving on Tuesday, going on holiday by the seaside for Christmas. There won't be another chance then."

Chrissie bit her lip. If she slipped away, she would lose her job at the hotel, perhaps end up back on the streets. But if she didn't, she would lose the only chance she had to have a family after all.

Princess Chrissie would take that chance. Her eyes stung with tears.

"I'll be here," she whispered.

⚜

THERE WAS no money for the omnibus this time.

Chrissie had left the hotel at four o' clock that morning, an hour before everyone would wake and start work. She'd slipped open the big window in the lobby and clambered out of that, closing it neatly behind her before dropping into the city streets and hurrying away as quickly as her limbs would carry her.

The walk had been almost intolerable. Her shoes pinched, blistered; the blisters burst, bled, and blistered again. The pain was appalling, but Chrissie kept going. Turning back now would be pointless. There was nothing to turn back to. She cried as she walked, and wanted to sit down and give up, go back to begging, go back to searching for work without any references, go back to living on the street. But Jonah's soft words in her mind urged her on. *Princess Chrissie.*

It was high noon by the time she left the outskirts of London and saw the Brentcliff house towering on the hill above her. Her body trembled with weakness; she had had no money for food, had eaten nothing since the night before. It was snowing hard, the day deep grey, and the house's windows were all golden with firelight, smoke tracing from its chimneys, black against the grey sky. That house held all the hope in Chrissie's world. She prayed the housekeeper would remember her promise. She prayed that the butler really was off in the city for his appointment.

Most of all, she prayed Carol and Floyd Brentcliff would want her. Tears dripped down her cheeks as she plodded up the long hill on her aching legs. *I never wanted you,* Dovie had said. Theodore had put her on the stagecoach and sent her to London.

But Nana Beulah had wanted her. Papa Roy had wanted her. Jonah had wanted her. And the strength of their love pushed her up the last few yards of that hill even when it felt as though her legs would drop off sooner than carry her all that way.

At last, she was knocking on the back door, and it swung open at once to reveal the housekeeper. Her eyes were wide, and she grabbed Chrissie's arm and tugged her into the blessed warmth of the kitchen, which smelled irresistibly of broth—

something hearty with beef in it, bubbling in a huge cauldron on the stove.

"What took you so long?" she hissed. "Thwaite is due back any minute now. And the master and mistress are getting ready to leave for the Gardiners' Christmas party."

"I'm sorry. I had to walk all the way." Tears filled Chrissie's eyes. "I'm sorry."

"Don't cry. It'll ruin your face." The housekeeper reached into the sink and gave her a warm, wet rag. "Rub your face—quickly now. Come. Come, we have to hurry."

Chrissie could hear the rattle of a carriage outside, being driven around to the front of the house. The housekeeper grabbed her hand and rushed her through hallways all hung with portraits and deeply carpeted. Finally, they burst out into a beautiful entrance hall. Chrissie gasped at the sight of it. There was a huge Christmas tree in the centre of it, gifts piled deep at its feet, all wrapped in bright colours and shiny ribbons. The tree was hung with gingerbread men and oranges and sweets, and a beautiful glass angel crowned the very top. She'd never seen anything like it in her life.

"Stand here." The housekeeper tugged her up to the tree, which smelled of roast chestnuts and pine, like Jonah did. She straightened Chrissie's dress, slapped down some of her hair. "Now smile."

"Will they love me?" Chrissie whispered.

"I think so. I hope so. I don't know," the housekeeper admitted.

A door swung open, held by a footman, and then Chrissie was looking up at her grandparents as they strode into the room. Floyd caught her eye first; he was tall and imposing, with a craggy jaw and piercing blue eyes, and he was resplendent in an emerald green suit with golden piping along the edges of his jacket and polished brass buttons. His eyes widened at the sight of her, and he whipped around to face the housekeeper. "Mrs. Carlson, what on earth is this?"

"Oh," gasped a voice.

Chrissie looked up. It was her grandmother. She knew it instantly, because the face was Nana Beulah's; far younger, less lined, yet holding the same depth of suffering in the corners of the eyes, the same powerful compassion in the set of the mouth. Carol pressed her hands to her mouth, let out a fluttering whimper, all colour draining from her face.

"Carol, darling." gasped Floyd. He grabbed Carol's arm. "Bring smelling salts, quickly."

"No, no." Carol sank into a nearby chair, upholstered in deepest red velvet. "No, it can't be. Oh, how I've prayed for this moment, though I know it to be impossible." Tears started to run down her rouged cheeks. She wore a beautiful, deep turquoise gown, elaborately embroidered. "Surely, it's not you, Dovie. Oh, it can't be you, my sweet, sweet Dovie."

"It's not her," growled Floyd.

"No, I'm not." Chrissie stepped forward, tears hovering in her eyes. "My name is Chrissie. Christmas, I mean. Christmas Ellis. I'm Dovie's daughter."

Carol gasped, covered her face with her hands, and sobbed wildly.

"Look what you've done." Floyd thundered. "Get out of this house at once."

Chrissie sucked in a breath of utter terror. "Sir..."

"Go!" Floyd shouted.

"*No*," Carol cried. She flew to her feet, her face smeared with tears. "No, Floyd. You won't send her away. You won't."

"We don't know if this is Dovie's child," Floyd barked.

"Of course, we do. Look at her. She looks just as Dovie did, when we—" Carol stopped. Then she rushed forward, her arms held out. "Oh, my dear, my sweet, sweet grandchild, come to me."

Then Dovie was wrapped in a perfumed embrace, sobbing in Carol's arms, her face buried in the silken folds of her grandmother's dress.

She would be home for Christmas after all.

CHAPTER 17

AND IN THAT ONE THUNDERCLAP, Chrissie's life was completely changed.

She sat in front of her vanity. Her *vanity*. She had never dreamed she would have one of her own; in fact, she'd only learned what they were when she saw them in some of the fancier rooms at the hotel and had to polish them. But a maid polished this vanity—a well-paid, well-fed, happy little maid who greeted Chrissie in the hallways every morning—and Chrissie sat in front of it, staring into the mirror while a lady's maid brushed her hair.

"Your hair is so beautiful, miss," said the lady's maid, pinning back some of it with a beautiful pearl-encrusted clasp. Carol had told her that all these fine things had belonged to Dovie once.

"Thank you." Chrissie smiled. "I can brush my own hair, you know. You don't have to."

"It's my biggest pleasure, miss." The girl's eyes gleamed with tears. "My whole life is changed now that your grandmother hired me from the workhouse two days ago. I hated it there, and she is very kind."

"She *is* very kind," Chrissie agreed. She smiled into the girl's eyes in the mirror. "I think we're going to be great friends, Becky. I hope so. This house feels very, well, *big* sometimes."

Becky's eyes lit up. "I would like that very much, miss. Thank you."

There was so much warmth and affection in Chrissie's life now. So very, very different from the utter loneliness she had endured just a few short days ago. And yet there was still a hole in her heart—a hole that only one thing could fill.

When Becky had swept up Chrissie's hair, beautifully soft and shiny now that it was washed anytime Chrissie wanted, and when she had finished buttoning the back of the lovely purple dress that fit her almost perfectly even though her skinny hips did not yet quite fill it out the way Dovie's had done, Chrissie headed downstairs. She paused, as always, to gaze up at the glorious Christmas tree in the entrance hall, all shimmering with baubles. There were so many gifts piled beneath it. Some of them were new; when Chrissie walked up to one of them, wrapped in shiny silvery paper, and turned over the label, she was startled to see her own name on the back of it.

Christmas presents. The last time she had had those was when Papa Roy had given her an orange, about a year before he died.

"Come along in, Chrissie, darling," Carol called out.

Chrissie headed through the tall oaken double doors and into the dining hall. Garlands littered the table, even though it was still several days before Christmas, and there was a delicious dinner being served by a liveried footman: golden pork chops, mounds of mashed potatoes, a whole tureen of roast vegetables. Chrissie was allowed to eat as much as she liked, almost for the first time in her life.

She curtseyed pointedly to Floyd, as always. He sat at the head of the table, staring at her. He had protested loudly when Carol had first said that she wanted Chrissie to come to stay with them forever, but they had argued heatedly in the study for a few moments, and Floyd had emerged defeated. Still, Chrissie longed for him to want her.

"Sit down, sweetheart," said Carol.

Floyd nodded to her, and this time, a small smile touched his lips. The footman pulled out Chrissie's chair, and she sat down on Floyd's left side, directly opposite Carol. A soft grace was said, and then the footman began to serve Chrissie her meal.

"How are you enjoying your explorations of the house, dear?" Carol asked, smiling widely. "I can't wait for summer. You'll just love exploring the grounds."

"I like it very much, Grandmother," said Chrissie. "I love being here. It's so warm and beautiful, and I think your Christmas decorations are just absolutely wonderful." She glanced at Floyd. "Thank you very much for letting me stay here, Mr. Brentcliff. I'll always be grateful to you."

This time, Floyd really did smile. "Call me Grandfather."

Chrissie's heart leaped. Not just because of Floyd's warm tone, but because of something else, too. Because of hope that the hole in her heart might soon be filled.

She ate slowly, relishing every morsel of the pork chops, relishing the feeling of eating without desperation and of knowing where her next meal was coming from. Carol chatted about the Christmas gathering they were attending that evening. "I know it's still almost a week before Christmas, but I'm getting so very excited." Her eyes shone. "It's so good to have a child in the house again. Someone to really enjoy it with."

Floyd glanced at Chrissie. "It truly is."

Chrissie smoothed the skirt of her dress, thinking of her mother. She'd told Floyd that she knew where Dovie was, the same day that she'd come here in the first place. They deserved to know. She couldn't forget the hollow expression in his eyes when he had told her that he knew. That he believed she was lost to them forever.

Where Floyd seemed hopeless, however, Carol appeared utterly determined to lavish all the love she had on Chrissie, as though she was trying to make up for Dovie somehow.

"We won't take you along to the gathering this time, darling," said Carol. "I know it would be very overwhelming for you. I would like you to stay here quietly, and rest. You know you can always ask Becky to read to you or show you some embroidery if you like."

"Thank you very much, Grandmother. I'd like that," said Chrissie.

"And of course, your dinner will be ready for you at seven, as usual," Carol went on. "You may ask for it to be sent up if you like or eat here."

Chrissie smiled at her. "Grandmother, may I tell you something?"

"What is it, dear?" asked Carol.

"Beulah and Roy would be very, very proud of you," said Chrissie.

Carol's eyes filled instantly with tears. She reached over the table and clasped Chrissie's hand. "Oh, bless you, bless you for saying that, you sweet thing," she gasped. "Bless you. I've come to learn that, however simple my parents' ways, they were good ways. I regret that I ... lost contact with them."

Floyd nodded, resting a hand on her shoulder. "And we both regret what we did to your mother," he murmured. His eyes held Chrissie's. "We will not make the same mistake with you."

Chrissie felt a blush rise to her cheeks, touched by Floyd's words. She lowered her eyes to her plate, wondering if she dare ask... but she had to ask, or the hole in her heart would yawn forever.

"Grandmother, I wanted to ask you something," said Chrissie softly.

Carol met her eyes. "Anything, dear. Anything."

"I had a friend, back in the village. A very, very good friend, and I used to write to him for years, but I haven't heard from him in a very long time. I didn't want him to know how far I had fallen, see." Chrissie paused. "I would like to write again. His name is Jonah. Jonah Costigan. I wanted to know if I might have your permission to write him again."

Carol's face went suddenly very, very pale, and she clutched at her heart.

"A boy?" barked Floyd, his face hardening again. "No."

"Grandfather..." Chrissie began.

"This is for your own good, Chrissie," said Floyd sharply. "I lost your mother to a boy. I won't—" His voice broke, and he looked away. "I won't lose you, too."

Chrissie hated the agony and fear she saw in her grandparents' eyes, so she ducked her head, even though her own heart throbbed. "Yes, Grandfather. I understand. I'll do as you say."

"There's a good girl," said Floyd.

Chrissie finished her meal in silence, trying not to let them see how sorrowful she was. They had given her so much. It seemed ungrateful to be so hurt over this, and yet that night, lying on her silken sheets, she gazed out of the chink in her curtains at the falling snow, and wished with all of her heart that she might be so bold as to pray for one last Christmas miracle.

CHRISSIE HAD NEVER in her life seen such a breath-taking wonder as Christmas morning in the Brentcliff house.

She emerged from her rooms to breakfast wearing a cheerful yellow dress she had come to love in the three weeks of her new life, humming fragments of Christmas carols to herself. When she reached the top of the stairs, a glorious sound filled the air: a piano being expertly played, teasing out the tune of "Joy to the World". The sound of it made Chrissie's heart skip. She hurried downstairs, Becky close behind her, and into the drawing-room to find Carol sitting at the piano, picking out the tune with expert fingers.

"Chrissie, darling." She laughed, her eyes shining. "Merry Christmas."

Chrissie ran to the piano and embraced her. "Merry Christmas, Grandmother."

Floyd was sitting in one of the armchairs by the fire, smiling widely. "Come in, dear, come in," he boomed. "I want you to open your presents."

Chrissie beamed at him. Her grandfather had mellowed even further over the past week or so, and it was beginning to feel wonderful in this home. More than wonderful: it was beginning to feel like *family*.

"What's your favorite Christmas carol, Chrissie?" asked Carol.

"O Holy Night," said Chrissie. "Nana used to tell me how she heard carollers singing it on the night that I was born."

Carol's eyes turned misty. "Then let me play it for you." She picked out the tune on the piano, and the soft notes filled the air.

The maids had brought the piles of presents from under the Christmas tree to the drawing room table, and Floyd grinned at Chrissie. "Go on, dear. Pick out a present."

"You first, Grandfather," said Chrissie. She lifted two small brown paper parcels from the heap on the table. "And you, Grandmother."

"Chrissie," Carol gasped, the song stopping abruptly. "You found presents for us?"

"You gave me a little money," said Chrissie shyly. "I sent Becky out to find them."

"Oh, darling, that money was for you." Carol laughed and kissed her, accepting the parcel. "Thank you."

The gifts were very small; a little ornate China dog for Carol, to join the collection on her mantelpiece, and a box of the hard-boiled sweets that Floyd loved for him. But both her grandparents wept a little and embraced her tightly.

"Now for yours, Chrissie," said Carol through her tears.

Chrissie gasped at her lovely gifts. They took turns, Chrissie opening one here and there from her grandparents, and her grandparents opening those from their friends. Soon a pile of wrapping paper lay all over the floor, and the room was filled with laughter. Floyd had given Chrissie a beautiful silver comb for her hair, engraved with her name; Carol had chosen a truly lovely pair of ice skates.

Chrissie gazed down at the skates in her hand. She wanted to tell Carol that she knew how to skate, that she had done it a few times on the frozen stream with Jonah, but the thought of Jonah made her heart throb with unexpected ferocity.

There was a discreet knock at the door. Floyd rose to his feet. "Ah, yes," he said. "That'll be your other Christmas present."

Chrissie looked up at him. "What do you mean, Grandfather?"

Floyd smiled. "Well, I looked into Jonah Costigan, after you had mentioned him." He cleared his throat. "Carol reminded me what consequences forbidden love had for Dovie. And you have been so good, and..." He stopped. "Well, everything I found out told me that he was a good young man. Not respectable enough to court you, you understand. But perhaps you could be friends, now that he's been hired to work in our stables."

Chrissie didn't understand. She stared at him.

"Answer the door, Chrissie." Carol's eyes were laughing.

Chrissie stumbled up to the door on numb legs and pulled it open. And Jonah was standing there. Jonah, tall and strong, with broad shoulders, his cheeks shaven, his hands brown and strong, his forearms sturdy, Jonah as a man instead of a boy, and yet the eyes were the boy's. The eyes belonged to her Prince Jonah.

"Hello, Princess Chrissie," he whispered.

And that was how all of their lives changed on one special Christmas.

EPILOGUE

ONE YEAR Later

IT WAS SNOWING in the stable yard, but in her fur-lined coat, Chrissie didn't feel a single kiss of cold. Clutching the precious parcel in her hands, she breathed steam in the cold air, and tiptoed over to the stable at the very end. As she approached, she could hear Jonah's soft voice rolling from the loose box, the way it always did. Jonah talked to the horses in a steady, quiet tone that stilled Chrissie's heart and calmed any fear that still lingered after all those years of suffering.

She peered over the half door and smiled at him. He was buckling a blanket around the chest of her own hack, a beautiful chestnut mare named Summer, since she had been

Floyd's gift to her when summer came. "Hello," she murmured.

Jonah smiled at her. "Come to visit your horse, miss?"

Chrissie giggled. "Oh, yes. I'm just here to say 'Merry Christmas' to Summer." She stroked the mare's satin nose.

Jonah grinned at her, leaning his elbows on the door of the box. Snow settled in his thick, dark hair, and his eyes held her entire world. Chrissie longed to throw her arms around him. But Floyd had told her many times that it would be improper to court a stable boy, that she had to wait.

Jonah must have read her desire in her eyes. "Not yet, Princess Chrissie," he said softly. "But soon. I'm saving every penny I have. Someday I'll have my own shoe shop, and then I'll be able to court you."

"Soon," said Chrissie, smiling up at him. "Tell me it will be soon."

"It will be," said Jonah, "and then, somehow, life will be even better."

"Our lives have already become a happy dream," Chrissie breathed. "I know you have to work, but..."

"I love the work, and the Brentcliffs are very good to me." Jonah grinned. "I don't mind the work for one moment."

Chrissie laughed softly. "Isn't it the most beautiful Christmas Eve?" She held out the parcel she'd held in her pocket. "Here's a toffee apple for you. I've saved your real present for tomorrow morning." She'd bought him a beautiful leather wallet, monogrammed with his initials. Carol had helped her. Carol didn't feel the same way about propriety that Floyd did.

"Why thank you, my princess." Jonah inclined his head, grinning, as he took it. He hesitated. "I know you wrote to your mother a few weeks ago. Have you heard anything?"

"Nothing," said Chrissie. "But I hold out hope I'll hear from her, change her heart. I've seen enough Christmas miracles to always believe in them now."

"Miss Chrissie?" Becky's voice called from the back door.

Chrissie looked up. "Yes, Becky?" She knew Floyd wouldn't stop her from visiting Jonah in the stable yard, but he had instructed Becky to make sure the visits were short.

"Your grandfather would like to see you in the study, miss," said Becky.

"All right." Chrissie stepped back. "See you tomorrow, Jonah."

"He would like to see Jonah too, please, miss," said Becky.

Jonah's eyes widened. "I hope I haven't upset him somehow."

Becky smothered a grin. "I couldn't say." She scampered off.

Jonah let himself out of the stable and they walked up the yard together through the snow. The house was utterly aglow with decorations. Inside its golden interior, bunting and garlands hung from every wall, and bright, shiny tinsel was wrapped around every rail and banister. Jonah marvelled at it open-mouthed as Chrissie led him over to Floyd's warm study, where leather armchairs surrounded a crackling fire.

Floyd was sitting behind his desk, holding a piece of paper and sipping eggnog. "Chrissie, Jonah," he said warmly. "Come in. Sit down." He led them over to the armchairs and sat.

Chrissie sank easily into hers, but Jonah swallowed. "Sir, are you sure?"

"Sit down, boy," grumbled Floyd.

Jonah perched on the edge of a chair, wide-eyed. Floyd studied them both, turning the paper over and over in his hands, too fast for Chrissie to see quite what it said.

"I was planning to keep this a surprise for Christmas morning," he said, "but, well, it's going to be busy and rushed, with church and all, and maybe I was just too excited to wait a moment longer." He grinned hugely.

"What is it, Grandfather?" Chrissie's heart thundered in her chest.

Floyd leaned forward. "I have watched you work in the stables, Jonah," he said. "I've learned that you are as honest as you are humble, as kind as you are courageous, and as hardworking as you are well-mannered. You are, in every way, the kind of courteous, chivalrous, self-controlled, temperate man that I would want to court my granddaughter, except in one respect." Floyd frowned. "You are simply too low-class for her. You own no property and have no business."

Jonah hung his head. "I'm saving every penny, sir. Truly, I love her. I will do anything for her, and I will find a way to become respectable enough for her, I promise you."

"You already have, boy," said Floyd. He held out the piece of paper to Jonah. "This is the title deed to a cobbler's shop on the outskirts of London, just a few minutes' ride from here. It's yours."

Jonah stared at Floyd, then at the paper, then at Floyd, then at Chrissie.

"Oh, Grandfather—" Chrissie cried.

"I have my own shop?" Jonah gasped. "I... I have my own shop?"

"You have your own shop." Floyd grinned widely. "And you may court Chrissie now. And you will start your business as soon as the holidays are over." His voice softened. "Merry Christmas."

"Oh, thank you, thank you," Jonah gushed, leaping to his feet.

"Grandfather, thank you." Chrissie rushed to embrace him.

Then she turned to embrace Jonah, wrapping him in her arms at last. Her every Christmas wish starting so many, many years before had now finally come true.

The End

CONTINUE READING...

THANK you for reading *An Orphan Called Christmas!* **Are you wondering what to read next?** Why not read ***The Ragged Seamstress?* Here's a sneak peek for you:**

Blanche Eplett worked the duster over the figurines on the mantelpiece in careful circles, whisking aside the tiny specks of dust that had gathered in the single day since the last time she'd carefully cleaned every corner of the study. She blew at a stray strand of hair that trickled down her face, then reached up and tucked it back under her bonnet before resuming her work. It was early afternoon, and she'd already worked nine hours, and she had another five or six to look forward to before her day was done. Her hands cramped, her back ached, and she wanted nothing more than to rest.

But she knew the Turners placed great value on these little trinkets, knew it from conversations she'd overheard while she was at work. The little ceramic elephant – the colourful one – had come all the way from India, where the original Ludwig Turner had first made his fortune generations ago. There was a glass case holding a series of war medals. None of them belonged to the current Mr. Turner (Ludwig the third, Blanche believed). Instead, his was the photograph in the frame that glared sternly out at her as she ran her duster over the glass.

She couldn't keep herself from hesitating a moment, running the cloth a second time over the glass, admiring the fine, strong lines of Mr. Turner's jaw and the piercing, noble expression in his eyes. The photograph had captured the fierceness in him, the sharp slant of his eyebrows, the height and definition of his cheekbones. But it had not been able to portray the other things about Mr. Turner that always made Blanche's heart flutter: the deep baritone of his voice, which always sounded as though at any moment he might break into laughter or song; the piercing green of his eyes, sharp and clear and yet somehow mysterious at the same time.

She was polishing the photograph a third time, unnecessarily, when she heard the creak of the study door. Starting guiltily, Blanche hurried to carry on dusting the mantelpiece. Not only was Mr. Turner the master of a fine household and she a mere housemaid, one whom he likely didn't even know existed, but he was married, too. He may as well have lived on the moon for all the access she might have had to him, no matter how his photograph made her feel.

"I'm nearly done here, Mrs. Boswick," she said quickly, knowing it must be the housekeeper come to check up on her. "I'll finish before Mr. Turner comes home."

"I'm afraid it's rather too late for that," said a warm baritone, smooth as silk against her skin.

Blanche whirled around, clutching the duster to her chest, a strange burst of both panic and elation running through her body. Mr. Turner himself was standing in the doorway, his hands buried in the pockets of his elegantly cut tweed shooting-jacket. He must be fresh from shooting pheasants with his friends; his boots were muddy, his wonderful chocolate-dark hair in disarray, and a fragrance of open air and heather emanated from him. It was all more enchanting than Blanche could express. She wrung the duster in her hands as though she could wring the feelings clean out of herself.

Click Here to Continue Reading!

https://www.ticahousepublishing.com/victorian-romance.html

THANKS FOR READING

IF YOU **LOVE** **VICTORIAN** **ROMANCE,** <u>**Click Here**</u>

https://victorian.subscribemenow.com/

to hear about all **New Faye Godwin Romance Releases! I will let you know as soon as they become available!**

Thank you, Friends! If you enjoyed ***An Orphan Called Christmas,*** would you kindly take a couple minutes to leave a positive review on Amazon? It only takes a moment, and positive reviews truly make a difference. Thank you so much! I appreciate it!

Much love,

Faye Godwin

MORE FAYE GODWIN VICTORIAN ROMANCES!

We love rich, dramatic Victorian Romances and have a library of Faye Godwin titles just for you! (Remember that ALL of Faye's Victorian titles can be downloaded FREE with Kindle Unlimited!)

CLICK HERE to discover Faye's Complete Collection of Victorian Romance!
https://ticahousepublishing.com/victorian-romance.html

ABOUT THE AUTHOR

Faye Godwin has been fascinated with Victorian Romance since she was a teen. After reading every Victorian Romance in her public library, she decided to start writing them herself —which she's been doing ever since. Faye lives with her husband and young son in England. She loves to travel throughout her country, dreaming up new plots for her romances. She's delighted to join the Tica House Publishing family and looks forward to getting to know her readers.

contact@ticahousepublishing.com

Printed in Great Britain
by Amazon

18467699R00139